There are harmless street people being killed and left on the clean floors all over the city in strange places. The places are expensive private clubs of spas, mostly serving women. There are no traces or fingerprints. The only thing in common is that a stray cat is found at each location.

But just as the city's best pair of detectives get involved, things get stranger. A very important executive commits suicide by shooting himself in the head — twice, and a cat is found waiting alone with the body.

Finally a reporter who's covering a bombing and the veterinarian lady who's having the cats isolated for the police are both kidnapped. Maybe it will take a touch of magic to get to the end of this puzzle.

Whiskers And Murder
Copyright © 2024 M. Garnet
ISBN: 978-1-4874-4273-6
Cover art by SudaGraphics Inc

Published by eXtasy Books Inc

Look for us online at:
www.eXtasybooks.com

WHISKERS AND MURDER

BY

M. GARNET

ACKNOWLEDGMENTS

This is the fifth in a series that
puts crime and magic into a mixture.
I want to thank the fans who have
enjoyed this unusual mystery series
and asked me for more.
Thanks, and keep reading.
This one is for My son-in-law, who
helped me with the details on betting
and behind-the-scenes information.
I love you, Hector.

I also need to acknowledge
the great creative work by
SudaGraphics, Inc.
for the distinctive covers that she
designs for each of my stories.
Covers DO sell books.

CHAPTER ONE

First on scene, the patrol officer looked at the raggedy, dirty man with the strange broken neck as he lay dead on the immaculate floor. The cops were writing up the scene as an irritated owner was trying to get the entire police crew out of the *Yoga For Heart* franchise. It was obvious that the dead man didn't belong at this location.

"He isn't a member and isn't related to any of our registered associates." The manager was shifting from one foot to the other, watching money slide away as her clients were prevented from entering.

A CSI worker, dressed in light blue clean protection clothing, picked up a calico-colored cat and looked around. "Whose cat is this? We have to get it away from the crime scene."

"It doesn't belong in here. Probably came in with that bum," the manager in her tight workout clothes commented.

A cop stepped forward. "I'll call Animal Control."

The CSI worker hesitated. "Make sure they keep it under quarantine. We'll need to have the vet check it for trace evidence." The guy covered in the blue paper booties handed over the very calm cat.

The cop smiled and cuddled the cat in his arms as he went out to find a car to make the call to get a pick up from animal rescue.

So began the investigation into another murder in this large city that would have more, maybe even tonight. Death was available among the poor and the rich.

Dr. Sarah Aggar had just finished the simple operation to neuter a beautiful Labrador Retriever that was someone's pet. She was pleased that the owner was being responsible. They had a citywide announcement of a free pet neuter process at any of the city's animal centers.

There was not much time in Sarah's schedule for operations anymore since she was now in charge of the entire program for the city. She had her office at the main center that wasn't in the center of the city. No one wanted a lot of animals in the downtown area, not with all the banks and high-end shopping.

The area where Sarah worked and the largest animal housing were located in the outer north district. There were two other centers. One was located on the west end, in what had turned into almost a slum area, and the other was in the south end near the river, but out in the suburbs with lots of room.

For reasons that Dr. Aggar didn't question, the city council was still being very generous in the budget for her division. She decided it wouldn't be good politics to starve poor animals, but it was okay to cut the pay for the police. She didn't understand politics but was grateful that she could buy plenty of supplies.

What she was disappointed in—was that the adoption of animals had fallen off. With the economy dropping down and a lot of people out of work, or their wages being cut short, funds for an extra mouth in the house wasn't on their list.

Still, she would give the orders to find room for strays and continue to encourage free procedures. Dr. Sarah Aggar knew she was a beautiful thirty-one-year-old woman who was married to a lot of mostly four-legged friends.

The expensive vans were kept out in the dark wet streets, saving the mistreated or feral animals and bringing them into the three housing facilities.

"Doctor, we got a call from the police. There's another cat involved in a murder situation." It was one of the many volunteers who approached her with the news.

Looking up as she was dumping her paper surgeon clothes, she asked, "Have the animal brought in here, and we'll keep it isolated."

"That means three cats in isolation because of crimes." The volunteer commented as he turned to leave.

Going into her office, she pulled out a couple of folders. There was the information of two earlier cats that were now stored in the isolation section that had been at a murder scene. She turned to her multi-leaf note calendar on her desk and noted that there were an even six days between each cat retrieval. Even more interesting, the cats had been found at a crime scene in different yoga studios.

Frowning, she had to wonder what police section was handling these unusual crime scenes.

Pierce Connors walked into his office and looked around for anything that would protect him from the anger that he knew was coming from his two bosses. He went to his desk and picked up the folder containing the information for the locations where they had the betting systems set-up. They needed a front that was the perfect cover for the back door rooms that accepted large and even small wagers.

The fuckin' cops had closed down most of the usual backroom places in the back of bars and the bookies at restaurants that were in rougher areas. Newspaper stands were now full of new people, as the old guys were suddenly behind bars, and street cops were everywhere. They were young cops, straight out of training and with stars in their eyes, and no way of getting into their pockets.

Now Connors had to find new places for waging dens, and he thought he had a strong idea that he'd put in front of the two people in the end office. He'd already started the process and was running into problems. He'd picked out somewhere new, where people went in and out at all odd hours. This would allow a back room where a wager place could be set up, and people moving at unusual times wouldn't be noticed. The good part was that this was a franchise with several locations around the city, and the owner was deep in over his head from his own betting habits. The bad part was that he wanted help in getting rid of a competitor that was doing better.

What Connors had to provide was additional funds to the loser, to allow him to hire some people to do some rough stuff around the competitor. Except the loser had employed something extraordinary, and what was happening was drawing some attention from the cops and the media.

His neck was on the line, and now he had to face the big guns without a bulletproof vest.

CHAPTER TWO

It was midnight, and the lights were bright inside the studio. Drummond and Smith had their gold detective badges on their jackets, as they got out of their car to slowly walk forward. Drummond knew they were a strange-looking pair that had an interesting reputation among a lot of the cops, who'd been around for a while. These two unusual detectives worked the night shift of Major Case Squad or MCS, and always seemed to solve their assignments.

They'd arrived before the CSI teams, and Drummond, the big one of the two, entered the double glass doors, he looked at the first officer. "Keep everyone back until I say." His voice was low, and the command wasn't to be questioned, so the officer nodded and began to give information on his shoulder mic.

His partner, Smith, was a tall, skinny man, who had a raincoat that seemed too large for his bony shoulders. He watched as Smith moved over toward the body of what appeared to be a street bum, stretched out on the clean floor. When he got close to the head, he put on rubber gloves and squatted down in an awkward position. With his long, thin legs bent, his knees were almost above his shoulders as he worked. As a determined detective, he was very fastidious and careful, bringing out a silver writing pen to lift back the dirty collar to see the man's neck. He also used the pen to push away the man's coat to get to the man's pockets. From Drummond's vantage point, they seemed empty. This street beggar had nothing.

As Smith worked at the dead man's side, Drummond was slowly making a circle around the body. His dark gaze sought something hidden under these bright lights on this clean, polished floor. He examined everything—the blue mats on one side, the covers over the AC vents, even the many electric sockets. One time, he went down on a heel, and his head went back and forth between the heels of the body and the outer doorway. It made the officer covering the door uncomfortable enough to move.

At last, he walked over to the person he assumed was the manager of this yoga studio. "Are there cameras near the body area?"

The lady shook her head. "We only have cameras over the counter. No one wants to be seen while doing their special moves or meditations."

The lean detective finally stood up, pulling the blue gloves from his hands. He looked at Drummond, and the big man nodded. They were evidently through with their part of the examination of the death scene.

As they walked toward the glass doors to exit, Drummond nodded at the officer guarding the area. "Let CSI and the coroner in now. We'll file our report back at headquarters."

Detective Hermon Smith and his large partner, known only with one name as Detective Drummond, walked across to their car. It wasn't the typical dark undercover car from impound. It belonged to Drummond, who'd purchased it from impound. They had permission to use it on official business. There were some people, including some of the officers in blue, who admired the deep red 2019 *Dodge Charger*. It had been upgraded, not that there needed to be much done to the built car initially. The heavy rear end with wide tires in the back and the big *Hellcat* engine made it a true monster on the city streets.

These two detectives operated differently from most people who'd worked their way up to that position. Hermon was a puzzle master who loved computers and could hack into anything or anywhere.

Drummond was able to fight his way out of any outnumbered bar brawl without a scratch. He saw details that weren't there for other eyes, and he believed in real magic. In fact, in the occult circles, he was known as a master wizard. This area was the one where the two friends disagreed, as Hermon couldn't believe in magic. He believed in black and white. He needed to see it in bits and pieces on his computers. Still, he was always surprised when his partner pulled out something surprising from his back pocket.

Hermon, even being a skinny nerd, had a gorgeous wife that would put most *Play Boy* models to shame, and the big, handsome Drummond lived with a fat black cat. *Go tell.*

Getting into the car and hearing the purr of that impressive engine, Drummond asked him the first usual question as he drove. "What did you find?"

This was their usual routine, and most wouldn't understand how they worked so closely together.

Hermon was starting up his computer, which was housed in a military-style metal case. "He was a man in his late forties, but looked older due to the life he led in the past few years. He didn't fight back, had no unusual bruises, besides all the ones from living outside without shelter."

His fingers flew over the keyboard as he hacked into the studio's camera. "His neck was broken in one quick, harsh twist of the head. It took someone with a lot of strength. I think it was done right where we found him. What did you find?" This was always the way the two partners worked — question to question to each other and quick answers.

Steering the car confidently, Drummond shrugged. "There

were no drag marks. There was no dirt, even though his shoes had street debris. It was as if he'd been lifted and transported to the spot where his head was twisted. There were two electrical outlets with burn marks."

Now Hermon stopped for a moment. "So, we have a real mystery."

"Yep, and this was not the first. It was the sixth." Drummond pulled in behind the big old building that was now the city's police headquarters.

"Got it, and I need to start a spreadsheet of all six." Spreadsheets and puzzles were what Hermon did best.

They parked at the back of the building in a special spot near one of the back doors. They were taking the back stairs to the second floor that housed the work area for detectives. On the night shift, there were very few people working with even some of those out on assignments. For reasons that were hard to understand and explain, these two detectives were in a side office that was usually only for captains or special officials. With the crimes these two had solved in the last year, no one was going to question the fact that they deserved the office.

As they entered, Hermon settled down in front of a group of computer screens and turned on the towers under the desk. Lying among all the folders was the main city's newspaper, which had embarrassed the police department. There was a lack of communication across the branches because the city was so large with so many different locations for the different sections of police divisions.

It was a reporter for the main newspaper that put together that a serial killer was dropping dead men in yoga parlors.

The Poor Are Neglected Again the headline read, as the report was more on the death of poverty-stricken people being ignored by the city officials than about the type of attacks on the dead men. Now that the police had several strange deaths on their hands and many politicians angry, the whole mess landed on the desk of these two detectives. To their surprise, the fourth crime had been committed on their watch.

Putting some dates up on his spreadsheet, Hermon was mumbling. "It's March, and the cold rain is drawing the homeless to look for warm places to sleep. Can you read me the dates of the different deaths, please?"

Drummond pulled out some folders, opened the first one, and began to give him the dates. "March third." He opened the second fold and read, "March nineth." The next folder was open, "March fifteenth."

"Okay, thanks. So, the last one is today, March twenty-first. We have no identity on any of the men yet. We need to check with the coroner and forensics."

Turning, Drummond leaned in to look at the screen. "Hermon, look at the dates. A death exactly every six days."

"Wow, partner, we have a killer with OCD." This was from him, who had all his pencils in a neat row and every button on his shirt neatly buttoned up to the neck.

Using the landline with the speaker, Drummond placed a call down to the forensics department first. "This is Detective Drummond. We need to know if you have anything on the three previous deaths in the yoga studios?"

"Yes, Detective, this is Technician Smigelski. We now have all the reports from the other divisions. Sorry to say that there isn't much to report. This killer's a real pro. No trace evidence at this time." There was a pause before the tech continued. "Of course, the crime tonight is still being processed, and since it's entirely under our jurisdiction, we have more control. Give us a call tomorrow, and we might have something to report."

"Thanks, Smigelski. Can you send copies of the other reports up to fax two-nine-one?"

"Will do. Bye."

"Better put the extra paper in the fax machine." Hermon bobbed his head in the direction of the area of the machines and paper storage in one corner. Since moving into this space, they'd slowly maxed it out to suit their needs. That eliminated using the machines out in the main large room.

Drummond's next call was to the coroner's office, and of course, he got the same results. The reports from the other divisions were ended, and the bodies were being transported over to the morgue here at headquarters. The body from the current crime had just been brought in, and there was no report as of yet. Yes, all reports could be faxed immediately or when an aide was available.

The fax began spitting out paper, and Hermon's long fingers flew over a strange-looking keyboard. Drummond reached over and grabbed some of the prints. He sat down and put his big motorcycle boots up on the back counter, as he began going through the papers. "Don't forget the cats, Hermon. We'll have to talk to the vet to see if there are any forensic traces we can get from the felines."

"Thanks. I need to add them to my spreadsheet." Hermon was very happy as he created puzzles for Drummond on the different screens. They might be unusual cops, but they were the best.

CHAPTER THREE

The cell phone on her nightstand woke Sarah up. As she rolled over to pick it up, she could see the time on it over one of the volunteers' names.

"This is Dr. Aggar."

"Dr. Aggar. There's been another of those strange police problems, and there's a cat involved. They want us to pick up the cat."

Sitting up in the dark room, Sarah tried to make sure she was awake enough to make sense as she spoke. "Okay. Have the cat carefully picked up and brought to my location. Keep it in isolation, and I'll take a look at it in the morning. Could you give it some water, but nothing more? Can you handle that for me?"

"Got it, boss. I'm in the roving van. I'll get over there right away."

"Thanks." Sarah hung up and put the phone back down. Maybe she could get a couple more hours before getting up to go to work. She rolled over a couple of times, then sighed and just threw off the covers. There would be no more sleep.

Getting up, she decided to get a long hot shower and stop for breakfast on the way to work. She had many animals to look after, and one special cat needed to have its hair combed for trace evidence. It would also need its teeth and its claws cleaned for the possible discovery of items essential to the police. It was hard to tell what a feral kitten could report when carefully handled.

Connors gave a little kick at the carpet as he walked back to his office. He not only still had his job, but he was also still alive, and he'd gotten approval for a larger budget to expand his idea on betting bases. The two people in that big corner office were strange, but they led the largest conglomerate of businesses in the state. He knew they had a couple of state senators in their pocket and were looking to back a U.S. Senator for more power.

On the other hand, they made an odd pair. The office was unusually large with floor-to-ceiling glass windows on the two outside walls. The surprising part was that for such a large office, there was very little furniture. In the corner of the glass window was an unusual triangular desk. Behind one side sat a woman, and behind the other side, sat a man. The long, straight edge of the triangle faced anyone who came into the office. It had only one straight chair before it, a seat without arms and thin padding. There was nothing else in the room, no more chairs or couches, and nothing was hanging on the bare wooden walls. Connors felt like there was an echo in the strange office.

Nothing was more bizarre than the man and woman who ran so many corporations and influenced many people. She would be almost called an attractive older woman. Except she had a burn scar on one side of her face. When in public, she wore veils or hats that covered that side. Here in this office, she frowned and let her minions see her anger with her damage.

As for the man, he'd never been close to being called handsome. He was obese beyond description and sat in a custommade electric chair that moved him everywhere. Between her glaring black eyes and his small beady ones, Connors always felt he needed a bath when he left their presence.

But he left with a larger budget and wouldn't have to

return as long as nothing went wrong. He didn't tell them he was running bookie offices. He was determined nothing was going to go wrong. He would go back to his street people and see that the people would be interested in his gyms and not the competitors' studios.

He went down two floors to another office that was also his. Here it was his working place. There was an aide outside, but she was smart and did her job. She took all his calls and left notes in the right order for him to pick up as he went past.

She never said anything, just nodded and held up a couple of folders; one was red, which was the critical issue he needed to address first. Connors took off his good watch and replaced it with a cheap brand. He changed into a suit from off-the-rack a standard store and put the expensive one on hangers in a closet. He finally ended up with older shoes and grabbed a coat he'd bought from the local thrift store. He'd changed from an outfit that had cost thousands to something that had been purchased with the change in his pocket.

He grabbed the red folder and went out the side door of his office and down the back stairs. After about three levels, he went in and took the elevator to the basement parking level. There, he went down below the level of the executive parking to where the people who did the common work parked their cars. He found a six-year-old sedan, pulled out his keys, and drove it out into the dirty, rainy streets. He needed to meet with a contact he had who knew people on the streets. People who would do anything for a small amount of money, and if he added more money, they would do unspeakable acts.

Well, he had a lot of money now, and he needed some acts that were beyond what he could describe. Of course, it was raining when late afternoon came over the city. The old sedan had plenty of gas to take him away from the center of the city and down south. At last, he turned east towards the river and the old section where everything was still run down, and no one was doing any repairs. This was the place where even the drug dealers stayed in their cars, and bums slept inside burnt-out buildings.

Drummond and Smith had a real problem, and it involved a newspaper reporter. The coroner here at the larger morgue had been able to identify the body of the second murdered homeless man. The very next day, the identity had been announced in the city newspaper.

The head coroner swore that it hadn't been announced, and there was an in-depth investigation to find the leak and seal it tight in his department. It wasn't the importance of the man's identity or the problem of the head coroner, but the captain decided that, as the detectives in charge of this crime spree, they needed to be involved. He wanted them to talk to the reporter and the people in the office downstairs.

Actually, the morgue was in an attached building. It had the standard entrances through the outside streets and a walkway behind the buildings with connected parking areas. But there was also a large underground passageway that allowed a lot of traffic between the two basements.

The public wasn't supposed to use this passageway, but attorneys, families, and some smart reporters would slip through this underground walk when it was raining heavily outside. Most of the cops, and even the guys in back in the repair and maintenance would use it to get somewhere quick and dry.

First, Drummond made sure Hermon was in the right hallway to the interrogation rooms. Hermon had a knack of getting lost in the basement of the large building that housed police headquarters.

His next move was to wander down the wide underground connecting hall. He'd gotten word from a worker in the coroner's department that a certain reporter was heading over after asking some questions in their area. The wait wasn't long, as there weren't many moving back and forth at this late hour. Drummond saw the man in his late forties and looked down at his pad, making notes as he walked. Evidently, the man was familiar with this hall and comfortable with the direction he was taking.

While rising from the wall Drummond was leaning against, he tossed the wooden match from his mouth. It arched and flashed into a flame but put itself out before it hit the corner drain. Just as the reporter came up even with him, Drummond turned and took hold of the man by his upper arm.

"Hey, what gives?" The reporter started to resist.

Holding up his badge to the couple of people who hesitated at the man's loud comment, he also put the badge in the reporter's face. He pulled the man forward in the direction the man was going and where he knew Hermon was waiting.

"You know I'm a reporter for the *News*. I'm getting information on a report for my editor." The man was struggling, but his resistance was useless against the big detective.

"You know this is interfering with a federal law, don't you." The man had finally quit resisting and was grasping his pad with both hands as he spoke.

"You're being held on trespassing. This is a restricted hallway." Drummond's voice was a low rasp, and it did shut up the man as they turned into the first hallway of the basement of headquarters. The reporter was smart enough to know exactly where they were and looked at the metal doors on one side.

"Hey, trespassing's not a felony. I'll pay a fine and go back to my office." The man looked around as Drummond opened one of the doors. Smith was sitting at the end of a long table with his impressive small laptop.

There was a stack of chairs in one corner, and Drummond pulled one off to sit it at the other end. "Have a seat." He indicated the chair and finally let go of the man's upper arm. "Got any ID on you?" Drummond asked as he stepped to one side of the ugly metal table.

The smell in this room was as bad as the old table. Too many people who'd been in here had either thrown up or urinated during questioning.

"Sure." The man pulled out his newspaper ID and then hunched over to get a wallet out of his back pocket. From the wallet, he pulled out a state-issued driver's license. Looking at the two small rectangles, Drummond nodded and slid them down to his partner, who began to type.

"So, Mr. John Wilhelm, you've been a reporter for a long time. You have your own column in the *News*." It was almost a statement from him.

"I've worked very hard to get where I am, and I do a great job, so you won't find fault with what I've done." The reporter, Wilhelm tried to puff up a bit.

Looking up over the back of the computer, Hermon smiled. "No, you've done a couple of exposé pieces that were excellent. You got some of the right people put out of business and behind bars. That's not our problem."

"Okay, okay." He turned in his seat to look at Drummond, who was leaning against the grey block wall behind him. "So, what's this all about?"

CHAPTER FOUR

The cat was inside a cardboard box that was lined all in white. Sarah had found what had finally settled the feral animal down into a purring feline. She was slowly brushing her with a special brush. The brush had many metal bristles, but each tip was covered by a tiny dot of rubber so that it messaged and didn't scratch.

As she slowly drew the brush through the hair, untold bits and pieces of everything that had collected on the fur for the last few days littered the white box. That also included the dead fleas and their eggs from the brief exposure to a gas spray, preparing before the brushing. The rest of the items were unnamed at first and would be turned over to the police for their experts to go through and identify. Tickling the girl under her chin, Sarah could get her to roll over to get her stomach and legs brushed slowly and carefully. That was where most of the debris was found.

Once the cat had been brushed clean and the white box was dirty, Sarah coaxed the cat into a soft net bag that left her head out. She'd already clipped her claws while she was quiet from the brushing, but she would hate the bath like all cats. Oh yes, her screech could be heard past several rooms, and it got some cries in reply. It didn't last long. Sarah had a volunteer helper get the cat in the net bag, and it was soon lathered, then rinsed, and warm air-dried.

"Okay, seal up the box and call the police so that they can pick it up for their forensics department." Sarah gave the instructions along with the box to one of her favorite helpers.

Now Sarah had a lot of paperwork to get to in her office, and she had the other cats that had been at other murder scenes but had been cleaned before being processed.

One of the other young vets stuck her head in Sarah's office. "Hey, I brought you a salad from the place across the street."

"Wow, that's great, Ginny. Thanks. What do I owe you?" Giving the girl a grateful nod, Sarah reached for her purse.

The girl smiled and moved some files to make room for the container. "You can pick up the next one. Hey, are you going to the meeting tonight?"

"No. I have another surgery to remove a tumor on a Retriever and then finish all this paperwork." Sarah shook her head.

"Damn, lady. You're married to this job." The young vet shook her head as she left to find another place to eat her lunch. Sarah's days went fast because she was doing what she loved. The problem was she loved working with the animals and was frustrated with all the paperwork that accompanied her job.

The estimate of work was correct—she was going to be late. She would get a bit of supper very late at a local deli. First, she got up and made a check on the large hospital. The city had been generous in providing for this habitat for the lost animals of the city. It seemed it was always good politics to get the budget to have an amount to set aside and brag about to keep and help the dogs and cats.

The surgery center was closing down at this time of day. The younger veterinarians did a lot of the less critical work and most of the neuter requirements. There was a room attached where the animals could recoup with constant care. The paid aides and volunteers stayed in this divided room around the clock every day of the year. Any hospital in the city would be envious of the clean white walls and sterile tables with containment sections. They had antiseptics and disinfects by the gallons in storage rooms.

Sarah was checking on the surgery rooms that were being closed down and prepped for any emergency that might be brought in through the night. Walking through the recovery rooms, she smiled and nodded at the people who were just finishing the last of their shift. There was a procedure for the change-over to make sure there was always enough to take care of the comfort for the injured.

Finally, Sarah went through a sealed door and down a long hallway. She was now entering the isolation zone. There was another closed door at the other end of the hall to let her into an area with sealed wall units that could hold animals of all sizes. This was where they could hold animals that were being treated for contagious diseases. Here was where the six cats were being held for the police because the poor felines had been at the scenes of murders.

Sitting in a parking lot of the big box store, Connors looked over at a similar older sedan car that pulled up next to him. The guy got out of the car and opened Connors' passenger door to slide in to make himself comfortable.

"Can I smoke?" the man asked as he pulled out a box of cigarettes.

"Sorry, my wife will smell it on my clothes." Connors held out what one would assume was a wad of money wrapped in a tan envelope.

There was silence as the guy tucked the envelope away without checking it.

"So, do you want another one? It would scare the people away from those fancy places real good." The man turned to face Connors, a bit of greed showing on his unshaven face.

"I have to think about it."

"Fuck. What's to think about?"

Connors frowned. "I'm not too happy about how your people did the deed. Who did you hire for the job anyway?"

"Hey!" The man fiddled with his hands. "You said to do something that would scare off the fancy folks. A bum from the streets bringing in dirt seems like a good mess to scare anyone."

"A bum, yes. But what the fuck are the cats about? And each bum on a special day, don't you think the cops will figure it out as some message? Your fuckin' guys are creeps." Connors was almost yelling in the closed-up car.

"Hey, calm down. They did the job." The two men sat for a few minutes in the car and watched the people pushing the baskets from the store to their cars. The rain was starting again, and the sound on the car's roof was a soft drumming. The two watched the shoppers pushing the carts faster, as loads were shoved into trunks and carts were left alone in parking spots. The inside of the car was beginning to smell damp.

"Okay." Connors' voice was calmer. "We can let this go for now. I'll meet you later at the usual place, the deli, and I'll have another place for you and the team to put on another show."

There were no handshakes, but Connors did smile as the two men sat and listened to the rain. It wasn't as if they were friends now. It was at least some peace between them.

At last, the rain let up, and the man nodded. "Well, boss, I need a smoke. I'll see you later." He got out and changed cars, and Connors used the time to drive away finally.

Connors now had another appointment. Doing all of these things that his bosses expected of him was often done off the books and off the clock. It came with the territory and the big checks. Money in his pocket was important to him and his lifestyle. He could relieve his conscience with funds in the bank.

While Drummond leaned against the wall and Smith played with his fancy portable computer, the reporter sat and smiled.

"You know, guys, I really had a good reason for being in the building. I had a chance to talk to someone who was just arrested."

Looking up from his computer, Smith shook his head. "You have an outstanding parking ticket."

Moving forward, Drummond laid the ID's he'd taken off the reporter. "Mr. John Wilhelm, a columnist for the City News."

The reporter turned in his seat to look up at him. "Yes, that's me. I'm often here at police headquarters."

"But you were in an area that's restricted to police or workers. It's clearly posted at all the entrances and several times on the walls of the underground hallway. You must've been aware that the bypass wasn't available for your use." Drummond stared at John without expression.

"I'm sorry. It was raining, and it was quicker." John just shrugged. He turned to face the skinny detective at the other end of the table. "I forgot about that parking ticket. I think it was right here on the street in front. I guess there'll be extra charges."

Pecking away, Smith shook his head.

"Well, you could lose your press pass for these two buildings." Drummond's voice was low but held authority.

"That would make a good column. Police prevent the press from some areas that are used constantly by all personnel. May I make notes on my pad?" John pointed at his pad that was lying near Hermon's computer. "Are you going to arrest me?"

"Do you have someplace to go besides the front desk

here?" Drummond stepped closer to the wall with the exit door.

"Yes, I'm a reporter. I already missed my chance to talk to someone you guys arrested. So, I need to make a stop at a great little deli and head back to my desk at the *News*. After all, I have a job to do also." Now the reporter was starting to act a bit antsy.

Behind the reporter's back, Drummond gave his partner a head nod towards the door. Hermon shut his computer down and got up to go to the door. They both left the reporter by himself in the dismal grey block interrogation room.

To the guard on the outside, Drummond stopped. "Give him an hour and then turn him loose."

Now it was time for the detectives to go up to their office and look at their spreadsheet to see if they could fill any of the squares. Hermon was grateful that he could follow his friend until they got to the back stairs, as he was always lost in the strange maze of hallways of small rooms in the basement that was so busy.

At last, they were up on the second floor of the strange old building with its columns in front and unusually high ceilings on each floor. The enormous detective section was clean, with good lighting due to a false fire department inspection. Someone had sent a notice that the semi-annual inspection had been moved up with tighter restrictions, and the entire building had been improved. Everyone was happy, and the inspection still hadn't happened.

Hermon brought up his computer, and Drummond found a chair where he could put his heavy motorcycle boots up on the back table.

"You know partner," Drummond mumbled in his low voice. "The next death is due on the twenty-seventh. That's tomorrow."

"Well, that happened after midnight. So do we check to see if there's been a call from any of those studios?" Hermon was working on something that was popping up on two screens.

"I think we need to get the debris from the veterinarian. It was the only cat that was caught and taken directly to the main animal station. I understand the head of the entire animal center helped. She has her office there and does a great job."

Hermon pointed at one screen. The information for Dr. Sarah Aggar came up with details of her background. It was impressive. The driver's license came up, and the woman was attractive. That was a surprise due to the fact that those small photos were famous for making a person look bad.

Nodding, Drummond turned around. "Let's put in an order for a black and white to go over and pick up the evidence from the cat. We can have it dropped off at forensics. Maybe they can tell us why these cats ended up at the murder scenes."

"Looks like the street cops are busy." Hermon pointed at a notice of an explosion at a deli across town.

CHAPTER FIVE

"Didn't the reporter say he was going to stop at a deli on his way to the newspaper?" Drummond was standing up, reaching for his long leather jacket.

Shutting down his bank of computers, Hermon also stood up and grabbed his special portable to follow him out. They ran down the back stairs and were soon out on the streets in their car, lights flashing. Like many undercover police cars, the *Charger* had many hidden lights that could announce that it was a car to get out of the way of when turned on. The obvious places were the turn signal spots in front and back, which had LED red strobe lights in each spot.

There were small three-inch-long ETD lights attached inside the grill that would light up, as some were red and some were white. Larger ones were on the flip license plate that turned over to expose the lights. A pop-up string of lights looked like the flat lights seen on the top of new cruisers in the back window. Pulling down the front visors was the last touch with the bright lights that were also attached to them. Now the dark red cruiser was brighter than a lot of the black and white cop cars on the streets.

When they finally pulled up to the sight of interest, Drummond killed the lights, feeling there was enough glare with all the rescue vehicles on the street. The area was being taped off back further, as more and more debris from the explosion was being found on the street and the opposite building and sidewalk across from the deli. There were a couple of ambulances already on the street with another coming up on the other side.

Pinning their clip badges on their front collars, they walked carefully beyond the tape to see the damage to the deli. Drummond approached a fire chief and nodded. The man was standing back, and it seemed like a good place out of the way to get the first details.

The two detectives just stood for a moment until the chief looked around and noticed them. "Yep, it was a bomb."

Nodding, Drummond let the man assume they were here to investigate the explosion.

"Deaths so far?" Drummond asked as he stepped closer to the frowning man.

"Structural damage hasn't been assessed, so we're careful that only my men are going in. They're bringing out ambulatory patients. So far, there's only one death directly at the site of the blast. That's not positive until the investigation."

A fireman was helping a woman out of the shattered glass front, walking towards them. He was probably taking her to the EMT truck where the heavy motor was running near them.

Holding his computer open with one hand, Hermon nudged Drummond. "That's Dr. Aggar, the vet who's in charge of the cats."

Nodding, Drummond left Hermon with the chief and walked over to the EMT truck where a worker was sitting the woman down. As Drummond got close, the emergency worker pulled out a large blue bag and began pulling things from it.

"Dr. Aggar?" Drummond asked as he tilted his head.

The woman looked up, and Drummond had to admire her strength as she shrugged off the worker's hands. She took the big piece of cotton and wiped at her face. She didn't look scared — she looked angry. At last, she looked over and up at him.

"Yes, and I want to get back to my animals that only bite and throw up or poop. What the hell's happening in this world?" Taking the bottle of liquid antiseptic from the intimidated worker's hands, Drummond took a large cotton pad, dampened it, and handed it to her. He traded it for the bloody pad that she was using.

"I hate to do this to you, but to get information, I need to ask questions immediately of each person who's able to talk. You seem pretty coherent. So what did you see, doctor?" He understood he had a strong person right in front of him who probably could tell a better report than most of the people who had experienced the explosion. Eyewitnesses were always a hit and miss account of what they think they saw. He knew that every person who was interviewed would tell a slightly different story — some would have no memory of the entire episode. To his luck, he was standing in front of an intelligent and angry woman who probably had a good memory of what she saw. His problem was that she might not have been in a position to see anything.

"I was going to the ladies' room and got blown into it through the door."

Drummond had his standard little notebook out. "So, you didn't see anything."

Dr. Aggar looked at the male EMT with the equipment. "I'm not going to the hospital. I got this from the sink when I was blasted into the bathroom." Then she looked at the detective. "A man in one of the front booths got a package from a courier. Who gets a delivery at a deli?"

"About what time did the delivery come in?" Drummond stopped the medical technician as the woman drew back from the man's attempt to apply some colored antiseptic. "I hate to bother you at such a desperate time, but do you remember anything about the delivery?"

The woman sat back down on the wide back bumper of the

EMT truck. She looked down at her hand, holding the cotton with just a little blood this time. Now she looked up at him and gave him a weak smile. "You look like a tough guy. Throw this med guy into his truck so he quits bothering me, and yes, I got a quick look at a small box."

Drummond nodded with a frown at the technician and caused the man to turn up his hands and step away. He decided this lady was too pretty to spend her time getting bitten and wiping up animal throw up or poop. "Look, I can get you out of here if you're sure you're okay. I can contact you later for further information."

She smiled bigger this time. "Just walk me past all these officials. My car's at the end of the block."

He offered a hand and made sure she was steady on her feet as they went past the emergency vehicles.

When they got beyond the yellow tape, she stopped. "The courier was in a brown uniform with one of those bright orange vests. He looked like he rode a bike." She nodded and turned to leave him, but added over her shoulder, "It's okay for you to drop by sometime later."

Okay, Drummond decided that was a must, as the lady was interesting in a lot of ways. He watched to make sure she got down the sidewalk past all the vehicles and cars and, finally, in the end, stopped at a dark car.

Turning, he went back to his partner. "Check for courier services that have bikers in brown uniforms and the usual orange alert vests."

"On it." Hermon never stopped tapping away at the portable computer.

"How many more were they able to bring out?" Drummond asked as he looked around at a few more injured people being treated.

Hermon looked up from his computer and gestured at another body that was being carried out. The man was alive and was put onto the waiting rolling gurney that two technicians had control of and moved away.

"Hey, isn't that the reporter?" Hermon pointed with his free hand. Two firemen had their arms together, and a man was sitting on them with his hands around their shoulders. It was obvious that his one leg was a mess. The pant leg was tattered and had been cut up, probably by one of the firemen. Blood was seeping down his foot as his sock and shoe were missing.

In approval, Drummond moved carefully around the chief and over water hoses. He could hear the chief talking, giving calm but distinct orders. The man was talking to someone behind the building, probably in the alley, making sure all the power was shut down in all the connecting buildings. The chief was also giving orders for a small amount of water to be put on a spot in the deli. Looking into the blown-out front of the eating and prep area, he couldn't see if there were any automatic sprinklers for the main section. There were sprinklers over the cooking area, and they were working.

Being careful not to step on anything, Drummond felt that ATF would soon be on-site to gather every piece of debris. They would slowly rebuild the bomb. It was amazing and fascinating how the whole thing worked with these ATF technicians. The detective finally reached the other end of the blast zone and the yellow ribbon, where several ambulances were sitting, waiting to help the injured. Following the gurney that went past the two closest big rigs, he went to one parked what would be called in front. Before they put the injured inside, a med-tech came forward to assess the injury.

By the time Drummond got close, he could hear the reporter arguing. "I need my pad."

"Just hold still. It looks like you're lucky. It missed the bones." The EMT was wiping the injured leg with clear liquid while one of the techs was trying to put standard belts over the reporter's chest.

Like the vet, the reporter was not co-operating. *Good, that means the reporter's conscious and clear-thinking.*

"Relax, Milligan, these guys only want to help you." Drummond spoke loud enough and with enough authority to get everyone's attention.

The reporter looked to the side and saw the big detective. "Fuck. You got my pad?"

Shaking his head, Drummond frowned at the reporter, "Nope, I bet that it's under the junk in the deli. Are you okay?"

The reporter snorted. "Like you care how I am. Look, I had nothing to do with this. What's even worse, I'm in the middle of the biggest news story for this week, and my back is turned. I see nothing. Damn, my boss is going to kick my ass down to Fashions."

"So, where were you sitting?" Drummond pulled out his small notebook.

"That's the problem. I always sat at the counter, but they cleaned up the seats, and Joy took me back to sit in a booth. The explosion pushed the back of the booth over me, and the only thing that stuck out was my leg." Roger reached down to pull the medic away from his leg.

The medic frowned. "She probably saved your life. Anyone sitting at the stools would have been killed by the blast." The med stated as he walked back to the truck.

Turning away, Drummond stopped with a question. "Did you know any of the people in the deli? I mean, any of the customers?"

Milligan flinched as the medic returned and began to restrain the injured leg. "I didn't look around. I was writing on my pad, and I gave my usual order to Joy, as I slid into the booth. The US president could have been in one of the booths, and I would've missed him. Hey, that's the leg that got hurt, easy there."

Giving up on the reporter, Drummond walked away. He was missing something important here, and he just couldn't put his finger on it. At that moment, one of the firemen came out carrying a very angry small wet cat.

"Easy, baby, I know you don't want to be in there with all that mess. Let me take you over and dry you off."

Damn, thought Drummond. There was that strange tie-in to the mystery, a cat. Now, to find out who got killed by the blast.

CHAPTER SIX

Deciding that they wouldn't get any more information at the blast scene, Drummond and Smith were back up in their office. They compared what they had on this particular crime spree. Both detectives knew that their captain would soon be looking for some answers, and all they had at this point were questions.

"We have big uncertainties with these crimes. Who did them, and why?" Drummond was looking at his notes on what he'd written down at the deli bombing.

"You think the deli bomb was connected with the killings at the studios across the city?" As usual, Hermon was working on his computers.

"Yep." Drummond's answer was terse but positive.

There was silence for a few seconds, and then Hermon quit typing. "Wait, you're saying that the bombing had something to do with the homeless getting killed at those studios? What ties them together?"

"Cats." Drummond held up his cell and showed a photo of a fireman carrying a cat out of the damaged deli restaurant. "In fact, I'll be late for the next shift. I think I'll go meet up with an expert on cats."

They discussed the fact that he left Hermon to work on his computer. He would hunt through many of the private sites he hacked into for information. He would also check on the couriers and the color of the deliverymen's uniforms. It would keep his fingers busy for quite a while.

Sarah had to take two tablets to get to sleep, but she wanted to be in the hospital for her animals early the next morning. Unfortunately, she woke up with a headache and delayed reactions, all due to a type of hangover from the pills.

By the time she had a long hot shower and got some coffee down, the fifteen-minute drive to the animal shelter seemed to take an hour, and she was late.

She did her usual rounds of the large facility. By the time she talked to everyone and saw the more critical situations, including one recovering and one dying pet, she finally made it to her office. There she started going over the folders of new admissions. The very first one was the cat that had been in the same circumstance she'd been last night, the bombing of the deli. Sarah had a double small piece of tape along with the beginning of the bruise on her forehead.

She hit one of the buttons on her phone that brought her in contact with a part of the hospital. "If Dr. Patton is available, I'd like to see him in my office."

It was only about two minutes before she heard footsteps outside her door.

"You needed me, Dr. Aggar?" A tall young man, who was one of the vets that her budget allowed her to hire, was now at her office opening.

"Hey, Bobby, there's a new cat in isolation. It's from the deli bombing. I need to put it into a white box and brush it to save any details. We'll send the box over to the police to their forensics division. Can you handle it for me?" She looked up at the young athletic man who looked like he should be out on a football field and not carefully working to save animals.

"Sure thing, boss. Glad to see you're okay. We all heard you were at the deli, so we were worried until we got word that you were fine. I'll take care of the cat. Let me know if there's anything else I can do." The young man was gone with a nod, and Sarah had one folder to put into the done basket. Now to work on the rest of the big pile — that brought out a big sigh. She would've preferred to be working with the animals.

Ever since she'd been promoted to head of the city's Animal Services, she spent more time either in her office or at City Hall meetings.

At noon, Marissa brought her a salad and a large iced tea. Marissa was their receptionist and accountant at the front counter for this receiving area. It was a busy area, as there was a lot of lost-and-found activity along with normal pet care for local residents. Marissa also had help from one aide who served at the window and with filing.

For a feeling of importance, Marissa always took care of Dr. Aggar when it came to announcements, packages, files, mail, and meals. Late in the day, with Sarah's pile of folders slowing dwindling, Marissa stuck her head in and smiled.

"Sarah, you have a visitor." She held a plain-looking business card. "It's a tall, dark, and I want to eat him up, and not starting at the head. Yum."

Reading the card, Sarah shook her head at Marissa's silly remark. "This is a detective about the bombing. Can you send him back?"

"I'll bring him back." As Marissa went down the hall, she mumbled something about the detective *is* a bomb.

Parking the *Charger* in the large parking lot in front of the building marked Public Animal Shelter — he waited a moment in the car, as a man came out of a side door. The man was leading a large, beautiful golden dog. He opened the back door of an SUV to let the dog settle down on the back seat.

Once the man was in and ready to pull out, Drummond got out to go over to the main door and enter. His first surprise was the smell. It wasn't of animals. It smelt like a doctor's office, all clean antiseptic.

There was a loud, "Hello," from across the room. It came from a fancy metal cage. In it was some type of large bird that cocked its head and spoke again. "Hello."

The waiting room was large and had an abundance of comfortable chairs scattered around. Away from the door was a couple that had a small dog sitting on a chair beside them. They were waiting for an appointment. Next to the entrance door was a large waist-high window, and it looked into a busy office with two women. The walls were full of open files and a lower desk type of work counter that ran around the area. The counter held files and a couple of computers. One woman sat on a rolling office chair, but she got up to come to the window.

"May I help you?"

Drummond handed the woman one of his standard police business cards with his badge attached to his collar. "I need to talk to Dr. Sarah Aggar."

"Oh," the woman looked at him longer than she looked at the card. "Yes, just a moment." Then she left through an opening at the back of the work area.

When the woman returned, she came through another door that opened into the waiting area and smiled. "I can take you back to Dr. Aggar's office. We'll go back this way."

Nodding to the dog and not the people, Drummond followed the woman. He decided she must have a walking problem, as she threw her hips from side to side. He was surprised at the size of the hospital, while he followed the woman down halls, past the noises of workers and animals. Eventually, after many turns and deep into the building, he was shown into a room with the name of Dr. Sarah Aggar on the open door.

"Come in, detective." Dr. Aggar stood up as he filled the opening of her doorway. This was the first time that

Drummond got a look at the woman. He was surprised that she was beautiful. He had no hesitation of putting that title to her; her face was that of an angel.

Strange that he hadn't noticed it last night, in the flashing lights and the blood on her forehead. He knew that he'd been distracted — but he was surprised that he hadn't recognized this unusual appeal.

"Have a seat. Can I get you something to drink?" He heard her words but adjusted his swelling cock, as he sat down in the indicated chair. He shook his head as he took control of his body and mind. It had been a while for him to have any interest in a female, and the last one that he'd found alluring turned out to be the head of a crime spree. Since then, he'd found other interests and not looked for a woman. He had a job to do, which filled his life with his interesting secret — magic.

Then he knew what he was seeing in her. She also practiced the occult. Perhaps she used it to calm her animals. Behind her desk, on a shelf with all kinds of books in loose piles, was a figure of a cat. Laying his hand with the large ring on the desk, he said nothing but waited for her reaction. Sarah looked from the ring to his dark eyes. After a moment, she looked over his shoulder out the open door, probably to make sure they were alone.

For those who didn't practice magic, the ring was very large and had an unusual design. But for anyone who dipped into any cult, the ring gave off an aura that projected the strength of control and application that announced only a person of power could wear such a symbol.

"Do I call you Detective or Master?"

"Drummond is my name, and if it's okay, can I call you Sarah? Do you practice?" His voice was low and meant for only her ears.

Sitting back with the busy desk between them, she lowered

her head. "I belong to a coven. We only practice white magic and help others. But my time is now devoted to this department the city's funded. I practice the medicine I spent eight years learning, and I'm proud of what I can do. Not for the city, but for the deserted pets that are left on the streets."

"What was your reason for being in the deli at that time?" Drummond removed his hand and sat back.

Sighing, Sarah also sat back. "I'd worked late and just wanted a quick meal before getting in bed. It isn't that far away."

Nodding, Drummond took out his regular police notebook and pen and continued. "Go through again what you saw and remember from the time you entered."

Crossing her arms over her chest, she looked up at the ceiling. "I was lucky and got a parking spot just across and down the street. The deli's open all the time and always seems to be busy. They were cleaning the counter seats and had a sign that said *No Seating*. That wasn't a problem for me. I went to the counter and placed an order for their number three.

"A man was arguing with the waitress because he couldn't sit at the counter, but he went with her towards the back. I decided to go to the restroom while my order was filled."

Stopping and closing her eyes, Sarah seemed to be thinking as she reached up and touched the small bandage on her forehead.

"Take your time. I'm in no hurry." Drummond's voice was low.

Sarah took a deep breath. "I turned and almost ran into the delivery guy, who was getting a signature from a guy in the first booth. I told you the guy was in brown with an orange vest. I don't remember what the guy in the booth looked like. I didn't glance over at him.

"I thought the whole thing was strange. I went back through the tables along with the booths and was almost in the restroom when something blew me through the door."

Putting away his pad of paper, Drummond gave a small smile. "Did you see a cat?"

"Oh, the one that the fireman found. No. But we have it back in isolation with the ones from the other murders."

Sitting up, Drummond asked, "You have all the cats here?"

"Yes, we have an isolation ward, and they're all here. I handled the last one from the murder on the twenty-first. We cleaned it for debris that was sent over to the police department's forensics. I had the same thing done for the cat from the blast."

Standing up, Drummond looked around. "Can I see this isolation area?"

CHAPTER SEVEN

Watching the woman walk in front of him, Drummond had to admit he admired a full figure. The lady was in shape and probably did a lot of heavy work, but she did have a great hourglass contour to her full hips.

Again, he was made aware of this building's large size as they went through rooms and down halls. At last, they reached a door with warnings that entrance was restricted. They had to go through two airtight doors to enter a room that held animals inside cages.

Each cage was fronted by glass, so he assumed they were also airtight and held animals that wouldn't be allowed to contact others. At the end were seven containers at waist level with very contented cats. They were in warm homes behind glass with blankets. There were water troughs and small bowls of dry food. They were all clean, and he knew there was no vermin on any of them.

Sarah reached out to the last holding pen and touched two buttons representing a safety release for the door. Reaching in, she coached the cat forward and into her arms. It curled up in her arm as if a baby ready for its mother's attention.

"This is the one from the deli blast area. The vet I had assigned to clean it said it had no wounds."

"All seven cats are connected," Drummond spoke in a low rasp, as he reached out to scratch an ear. The cat immediately perked up, then jumped from her arm over to his shoulder. His reflex was quick, and he caught the cat to hold it to tickle its chin.

"Do you have a familiar, Sarah?" Drummond asked in a low voice, as he looked down at the cat in his arms. Drummond had been born into the ancient practice of the occult and knew that witches and those that practiced magic often had an animal close to them. These were called familiars.

"No. All the poor animals in this dark wet city are my close ones." She took the cat away from him and put it back into the container. It turned several times then found a spot to settle down on the blanket. It did look up and watch them.

Smiling at the cat, Drummond stated, "They're all female. They're not related. They're all involved with a crime spree, and the last one was the bomb at the deli."

Turning to look up at him, Sarah seemed surprised. "You think that this is all involved with witchcraft?"

"Whoever did this was very smart and left no traces, no fingerprints, no footprints, no cloth remnants, no skin flakes. Nothing but their one mistake, the female cats."

Stepping away from the front glass containers, Sarah shook her head. "Why the cats?"

Drummond raised a hand as if to encompass the entire room. "Cats are sensitive to psychic powers. They're welcomed into magic circles when the power for spells originates. When working magic, cats act as guards in psychic defense. But cats are also independent. They often don't leave, or they can just get up and walk away." He pointed at the one watching them.

It shook its head and then decided it had seen enough, and it began to clean its front paws, one after another. That was more interesting than the people who fed or tickled it in the right places. A cat would do a lot, but at its own discretion.

Glancing up at a large wall clock, Sarah shrugged. "The evening shift is coming on. There's someone on-shift all the time at this hospital. We have a vet to handle emergencies."

Drummond turned and seemed to see the exit. "Look, how

about I buy you . . . dinner?"

"Well, I don't think they'll miss me for an hour." Her voice had a short falter.

They went back past her office for her to claim her things. It was the type of effort women did and then they went out a side door without seeing anyone. He did notice she'd left a short note on her desk. It was easy to get around the building to where his car was parked. He talked her into letting him drive. He took her to a local brewery that served great steaks and their own beer.

Many would've been surprised that the two didn't talk a lot, but the quiet between them was comfortable. It was rare for the two professionals to find silence, but both had a life full of people and noise. Sitting with someone else who just smiled and commented on the good food was a nice relief in their hectic lives.

Afterward, they walked the dark streets instead of getting in and driving away immediately. Again, it was just the companionship that filled the moments for them that let them relax.

He took Sarah home, and she told him that she would get a ride to work the next morning to get her car. There was a kiss—it started as a gentle one on the top step by the entry. But the heat exploded, and it was Drummond who had to fight to pull away and look into those violet eyes. Like a coward, he turned and ran down the steps to get into the car. But he sat and waited to make sure she got inside safely. He shook his head as he adjusted his pants. This was a female he could get attached to very quickly.

Well, it was time to get back to work, so he headed downtown to headquarters to join his partner. Parking in his usual reserved place by the back door, he texted Hermon before leaving the car. *Any news*

The answer came back immediately. *Hi D. Check in with forensics about the blast and get their reports. Tks. H.*

Smiling, Drummond entered the big door and went down to the basement. There were probably some reports ready, but he knew Hermon was hoping someone else would come along to get the reports from the lower rooms. On the night shift, there was a lady who Hermon claimed had a crush on Drummond, and she got out all the reports fast and efficiently. The lady wasn't on duty, but the report was ready on a thumb drive. That would make Hermon happy since anything that would allow him to play with computers pleased him.

Now it was back up the stairs to the second floor and over to their special office where Hermon was working on his toys. He was either landing planes at the airport or checking the history on how to build small bombs. Handing him the small trinket, Drummond laughed as the item made Hermon smile.

Hermon plugged it into the front of one of the many computer towers hidden under the desk.

Hermon then took all the pieces in the different slides on the small drive, and he began to rebuild the bomb. Drummond had seen this activity done before and found it totally fascinating. This time, it wasn't the engaging form of a pipe bomb filling in on the screen. It was still lots of pieces that Hermon was having a lot of trouble fitting together.

"Problems with your puzzle, partner?" Drummond tapped Hermon on the shoulder.

"Yep. Whatever blew the head off of the guy that opened the box, it was unique." Hermon's fingers worked the keys, while additional small pieces appeared on the main screen. On two of the other side-screens were many bits and pieces that Drummond couldn't recognize. Hermon would pull a piece over to the main screen and move it around to fit it against something else. The box was already there, and some items were together, but it didn't mean anything yet. There were segments of red showing through what had been burnt.

"Wait," Hermon yelled, and Drummond pulled back to give him room. Hermon was searching on another screen and brought up a picture of a bar of dynamite. It was the plain old long tubes with the silly little string sticking out of one end.

"They built a bomb simply with old-fashioned dynamite. How did they set it off?" Drummond was looking at the screens as close as Hermon when he spoke out in surprise.

"Still building," Hermon mumbled. Now, things were beginning to fit together on the big screen. There were two of the old dark red color tubes of dynamite. There was some black electrical tape that was starting to fit together around the sticks.

"Where do they have the actual pieces?" Drummond stood up to pull out his cellphone.

"Over in building nineteen." Hermon was distracted, having too much fun matching minute pieces together.

"I'll keep in touch with you. We need to find something that has nothing to do with the bomb." Drummond was jogging over to the back stairs.

It took him fifteen minutes to get through the wide underground hallways to another building and then into the bomb laboratory. There, a woman in a protective white suit pointed him to a section that was handling the blast from the deli.

The first thing he did as he moved past the wide long metal counter was pick up a small round red cap and held it up. "This is the end of a stick of TNT. You can find all of two pieces."

Suddenly latex hands were busy.

"Can we help you with anything, Detective," another paper-enclosed worker asked.

"I'm looking for something that isn't connected with the bomb in any way."

"Oh, yes. We put those items down at the end." The man pointed toward the end of the long metal table with bright lights over the entire length.

Drummond understood why all of this area was full of odd items. There was a shoe, bits of pieces from the table edge where the bomb had blown, and long pieces of other debris too large to be part of the bomb. He walked around the end and was careful not to touch anything, and then he saw what he was looking for.

It was a small wooden box, almost a coffin, highly damaged, but someone had tried to fit the top and bottom back together. Near it was a strange piece of a root with blue paint in circles on it.

A wood witch.

CHAPTER EIGHT

Taking pictures with his cell, he was talking to his partner. "This is what the man picked up to release the striker switch."

Giving a nearby worker the instructions to bag the box and root then send it to forensics, Drummond started back up to the office. After twenty minutes of jogging and double steps, he looked for his chair and wasn't even breathing heavily.

"How did you get here so fast?" Hermon accepted the phone and transferred the photos.

"I hurried." Drummond pointed at the small box on the screen. "That's a special occult item. It's done by what's called a wood witch."

"Okay, partner, you know I don't believe in that shit. On the other hand, you've convinced me that there are idiots out there who believe in the silly stuff. It's like some cult religions. They practice odd . . . damn, I can't think of a word for what they do." Hermon had actually quit typing.

"Well, partner . . ." Drummond finally found his chair. "You're going to love this one. The root with its decorations on it was something created by a person called a wood witch. They can be a man or a woman. They put a hex on the wood and then put it in a box to preserve the spell until it's needed."

There was a snort from Hermon. "Tell me more about these myths."

"If a person believes enough, sometimes a myth can be harmful. The wood witch performs rituals by going into a state of mind. They fetch some branches from a special tree or bush and wrap them in a black cloth that's infused in henbane."

Raising a hand, Hermon stopped the lesson. "Wait, henbane's on the endangered plant list."

"Yes, but witches all over the world cultivate it in small hidden gardens. They're careful and sell the leaves, both fresh and dry."

Pointing at the screen with the root, Hermon got his friend back onto the information. "So, what does that have to do with this?"

"Well, if you believe in magic, then a wood witch would put a hex or bad magic on the bit of wood and put it in the coffin. The wood witch would send it to someone that the witch wished bad karma to and have it delivered to them. In this case, it was used as the weight to hold down the striker until someone picked it up. Lift the coffin, and boom."

With his fingers working the screen and moving the coffin over the two pieces of TNT, now Hermon nodded. "Whether you believe in magic or not, it was evil, and it did the job. Did the witch that built this bomb believe in magic?"

Putting his big motorcycle boots up on the back desk, Drummond nodded. "Oh, yes. He or she is a practicing wood witch. They're rare. They call on the sorrow, pain, agony, hatred, or rage to do their bidding. They would burn herbs of the daemon, inhale the smoke, and dance while they screamed. And in their minds, they conjured evil. They built the bomb and killed the man who opened the box when he lifted the coffin."

Detective Smith pushed his chair back from his screens. "Damn, that sends chills down my back. There are a lot of crazy people in this world. So, what do we do with this information?" Hermon looked a little lost.

"We go to the woods." Drummond stood up and grabbed his phone to stick it in the pocket of his leather jacket. "But we can do that on our shift tomorrow night. Let me take you home now. You have a lady to please, and I have a cat to feed. Tomorrow night, we witch hunt."

"Yuck."

With the strange words, both detectives were still happy as they had some answers, even if some were very strange.

CHAPTER NINE

Dr. Aggar was distracted as she watched some of the volunteers cleaning out cages, making them ready for new tenants. This was the wing of the big hospital where they accepted the rescued animals. Since most of the ones brought in were from the streets or held in mistreated conditions, they had to be cleaned and debugged first.

They were held for a day or two so that either Dr. Aggar or one of the other vets could check them out for injuries or diseases. This was always a busy section since there seemed to be an abundance of four-legged friends in need of a home and attention.

None of these hard-working people would ever understand what was driving Sarah's need to care for the critters that were brought in . . . wet, tattered, and hungry. Some could assume it was just a warm heart, and others would think that perhaps the head vet had witnessed the mistreatment of cats or dogs when she was young. Perhaps she had a parent or a neighbor who had the animals in unclean pens that weren't fed properly, and she learned about the heartbreak of endangered animals early.

They would be wrong. It was Sarah herself who'd been at the end of the hurt and lack of love within a house of misunderstanding.

For Sarah and her brother, Stan, they were only struck when they got in the way. They learned early not to reach out to the two emaciated pair of adults in the small dirty house.

Drugs had made the interest in sex pass beyond a need for the two people. The blessing was there were no additional siblings to add to the small amount of food to share. Actual food coming in was rare. It happened when the two people got hungry between the drugs and had pizza or Chinese delivered. They also picked up something they referred to as fast-food when they were out begging or stealing.

The two small children had to wait until the adults either fell asleep or were wasted in order to steal what was left of the food. It had been years since either of them had tasted warm or fresh meals. Like their parents, they began to look for things to steal. Although they were beaten if caught leaving the house, it was easy to leave when the adults were out cold.

At first, it was just going through the garbage of the nearby neighbors. Unlike their adults, who never cleaned or threw out anything, the neighbors had a garbage can that went out to the street once a week. There were small plastic bags of old bread. The two pulled off the green growth from the sides and ate the dry center.

They found pieces of cheese with grey fur, but it tasted like heaven when scraped clean. The stray dog that often sat on the back porch to get out of the rain, ate the bread's bad edges without hesitation. As they got tall enough to reach into the cans without turning them over, they went further down from house to house, grabbing shriveled fruit and sour milk in the bottom of containers. There came a time when the man and woman sat on a lumpy couch, and suddenly the thing was on fire because they were doing something that made them happy.

Her and Stan were sleeping on the foul mattress in a small room just off the area where the druggies were sitting. The adults were so drugged out they hardly felt the pain as the fire and smoke knocked them out. All of the windows had been covered with rotten wood since the glass was broken over the years.

When Sarah and Stan woke, the smoke was too thick for them to even see in the dark. In all the ugliness of Sarah's life, that night was the worst and the best.

The fire department finally broke in and put out the flaming bodies in the first room. By the time they found her and Stan and took them to the hospital, it was too late for Stan. He was a year younger than Sarah and had stood up to run into the other room. There had been too much smoke in his lungs for his young, thin life. Sarah had been found unconscious on the floor near the mattress. Being on the floor, she didn't get as much smoke into her, and they were able to save her.

It took them a year to find her a foster home. During that time, she hardly spoke and was behind others her age due to a lack of school, food, and vitamins. Sarah was frightened, angry, and resistant to any help. Miracles still do happen, and a woman who worked at the placement service felt the pull of her heartstrings. She took Sarah home just to give the child a break, and her husband enjoyed cooking for her since she was so skinny. Sarah had found a new and different home. It was a home of love and compassion and people who took time to let Sarah grow and understand that what had happened in her past wasn't normal.

Now Sarah helped poor animals from the streets because she remembered what it was like to be hungry and mistreated. She had a connection to each poor cat and dog that was brought through the doors of the hospital.

There also was no tolerance in Sarah Aggar's world for those who didn't take care of the ones they were responsible for, like pets or children. She'd gone to court several times to be a witness in cases of multiple puppy mills. Dr. Aggar was famous for going out of her way to shut down such places that produced the small babies to sell cheap. She even lobbied the state government for stricter laws for the shops that sold puppies.

In her view, the idea was to make sure that only babies that came from specially licensed houses should be available. Not only that, the license required constant monitoring to make sure that all rules were abided. At no time were the pets turning out too many births.

Sarah had proof that there were more dogs in this city than people. She offered free neutering whenever possible. Sarah wanted to make the offer a process free from the city, but she hadn't found any backing. There was still a large amount of people who felt it stepped on their rights. There was also the one group that she hated the most. They were the ones who raised and trained dogs for the fights. They claimed the dogs needed to be full and not neutered in order to attack.

The same approach was for those who raised and trained guard dogs. Even the police dogs were kept in their natural condition. That wouldn't be a problem if they were kept in controlled kennels where the breeding was something that was under a record. Sarah wanted to make sure that the breeding dogs didn't produce more puppies than needed, and then they would be castrated to live out their lives comfortably with a family.

The people working in the clinic didn't need the boss standing here glowering at them. Dr. Aggar forced a smile on her face and started back through the many halls to her office. Turning one hall, she remembered going down it with the detective. This time, she allowed a genuine smile as she thought about the large handsome Lt. Drummond. She did wonder where he was right now. She nodded at herself, remembering that he worked the late-night shifts. He would be at home asleep right now.

After such a long time of not feeling any attraction to men, she found it strange to be drawn to the tall man with a gold badge. Maybe it was time to take an interest in something else that didn't walk on four legs. When she got to her office and had some privacy, she picked up a special business card and left a message. She was glad that it was only a message. *Let fate decide.*

Drummond fed his cat and went out to pick up his partner, who'd been fed by his wife. They still had to go through a fast-food restaurant in order to stock up for the office. No matter how bad the coffee was at these quick places, it was better than what was in the big urns at headquarters. They parked in their special spot right next to the back door, where they went in and up the wide stairs to the second floor.

In their unusual office, Hermon started up all the computers with his special code, and Drummond sat down and dug out his cellphone to get his messages. He put the phone on speaker, and they both listened.

The first message was from the reporter Roger Milligan.

Detective, this is Reporter Milligan of the City News. I have a photo of the courier who delivered to the bomb site. As my due duty, I'll trade it for information. Contact me for a meeting.

"Due duty?" Hermon actually hit his keyboard. "He should just come forward and turn that photo in at the front desk."

"Yeah, that'll be the day." Drummond saved the message and went to the next.

This is Lt. Ronson, Detective at Station Five. My partner and I have an odd case that involves a so-called suicide where a guy shot himself twice with a snub-nosed thirty-eight. The reason we're reaching out to you is that the guy that discovered and identified the situation is a cat lover. Cats came up on the inner computer with you guys. Contact me.

The two partners looked at each other. "What the hell, Drummond? Are we now the cat detectives?" Hermon worked the keys and pulled up the information from Station Five about the suicide. There wasn't much since there wasn't any information from the coroner, and the CSI team hadn't turned in a report. The only thing on the computer was a short initial report from the detectives.

"Ever hear of a suicide shooting himself twice?" Drummond pointed at the screen. It was only one of the points on the report. Again, Drummond saved the message and punched in the last call.

Uh, hello, Detective. I'm wondering, oh, this is Dr. Aggar, Sarah. Uh, I was wondering about, geez. Sorry, I shouldn't bother you. I realize you work the night shift. Okay, I'll be working late tonight. This is silly. I'll be working late tonight, and if I can find a good latte, I'll be at home. If you have time, give me a call on this number.

This time Hermon had no comment as he began to work on a search on his computer for information on snub-nosed thirty-eights and their dependability.

Suddenly, Drummond got up and started for the door. "I'll be back later."

Hermon glanced up. "You going to see the reporter?"

Shaking his head as Drummond started. "No, I need to deliver some coffee."

It took Drummond ten minutes to find the drive-thru of the famous coffee place where he picked up a small latte and a giant black coffee. From there, he let the *Charger* do its thing as it passed everything on the streets, getting to a certain lady's front steps. He parked illegally and pulled down the passenger sunscreen that showed the police ID on it. Carrying coffee stacked in one hand, he went up the steps and rang the bell.

"Yes?" the sweet voice spoke through the speaker.

"Your latte delivery, madam." He used his detective's voice.

There was silence for a moment, and there was a shadow

movement behind the window in the door of the entry. Sarah opened the door and looked at him with those wide violet eyes. "Oh Damn, just what I need. I feel so embarrassed. Please come in."

He followed her into the large living room with a fireplace big enough to hold a full tree. There was a big flame in it to chase away the wet feeling from the rain outside. It was the warm, comfortable room that he went to as he entered. The woman was wearing a long soft wrap with a tie at the waist that clung to her figure as she walked in bare feet. He knew he was in deep trouble.

The first thing she did was to excuse herself as she moved her animals to another room. He was amazed to see that she had to carry a fat black cat that seemed too old to move. There was a large dog with a flopping tail but missing one back leg. The dog had no problem moving on its three legs as it followed her into another room. She stayed there for a couple of minutes before coming out and closing the door.

"Sorry, my pets are friendly, but I don't want hair all over you. I was just relaxing and working." She pointed at the room.

There was a stack of pillows on the floor on one side with a multitude of folders and paper around a laptop. This woman had been working on the floor. Drummond took a deep breath and thought he needed to get down on the floor with her. No, he needed to get her down on the floor. *Yes.*

Sarah started the conversation on a neutral point as she sat on one of the pillows and held up a folder. Drummond went over to a chair near her and traded her a paper cup for the folder. He was glad to sit as his jeans were getting tight in the crotch.

CHAPTER TEN

He was amazed as they talked and spoke of animals and criminals. They both agreed on the city's sadness and how it had deteriorated from its years of growth to its dark center now. Somewhere along the evening with some wine — a kiss had happened, and the kiss had turned into more. Now he had her where he could worship her. This was right, as he went down on his naked knees and held her legs apart to put his face in that sacred place. The smell made his member stand up and tremble.

It was strange that women went out of their way to hide this natural smell in this modern world. This was the female's normal odor that every man immediately reacted to and wanted to have in the air as they met each woman. Although she was very clean, at least she didn't cover it up with powders and perfumes. Now he sunk into that smell and wet area. If it felt good to him, he knew what would feel extra for her, and he took his tongue to that round hot ridge to draw it into his lips until she bucked and groaned.

He looked up over her soft mound and saw the full breasts hiding her thrown-back head. Yes, there was a heaven on earth. Drummond had a pleasant pain, needing his release, as he brought her to an orgasm with his tongue. Still, he would bring her all the pleasure he could before he sank into her, to adore her differently.

For Sarah, her mind and body were on a different plain. She'd never had a sexual experience like this in her life. She wasn't a virgin, but the times she'd followed through with a man, it was quick and an orgasm with him once or twice, but not what this big man was doing to her body. There was no time to think. There was just time to come down before he took her back up again. How could he do that? And it was amazing that he seemed to enjoy giving her joy. Oh, she felt the build of another spasm hit her body, and even her toes curled. She'd lost count, and it didn't matter. There had never been a man in her life like this one with the black eyes that gleamed with success, as at last, he rose.

Letting out a sigh, Sarah reached to feel the rough short-cut black hair. He moved up to run his tongue around her inset button and then continued upward. That wet tongue left a trail under one breast and then the other until he sucked a nipple into his mouth, and she had to close her eyes as warm pain shot down her body. Heat was past her stomach and into that wet place between her legs again. She was able to hold it off since she wanted something more this time.

At last, his mouth was on hers, and she tasted herself. He shifted his body without taking his mouth away and with a hand by her head—his other was guiding something important into her.

He slowed as he realized she was tight against his size. He drew back from the kiss to watch her face when he pushed into her. He wanted to thrust in deeply, but he wanted her to relax and appreciate every second of what they were doing. He felt he might have played with that special sensitive kernel too much, so he returned to her mouth, using it to bring them both to more heat. He felt her core relax, and he entered deeper and began the rhythm of the ancient dance.

Drummond had timed it perfectly as he pumped and

pulled her up one last time, her hot core wrapped around him with the veins standing out all over. Nature took over, and he dumped inside of her as her own muscles milked him over and over.

Finally, they both were exhausted, and he dropped down beside her with a leg and an arm over her body, both of them sweaty and breathing heavily.

Hermon looked up with a bigger smile than Drummond's as the big guy entered the office at three am.

"Guess what I got?" Hermon waived a picture printed from one of the machines in the office.

"How about you just show and tell me, and I won't have to guess." Drummond pulled a rolling chair out and propped his feet up on the back desk.

Handing over the glossy copy, Hermon explained. "I did some deep looking into the City News computers to see if the reporter had put anything there."

Taking a breath, Hermon tapped some keys while Drummond looked at the photo. It was of a courier for a bike delivery company. Drummond raised his eyebrows. "This company delivers all over the city at all times. What ties this in with the deli bombing?"

"Well, according to what's going to appear in a future report from Roger Milligan, this is a photo taken by a Mr. Donald Zepher. He saw this man parking his bike at the corner, taking a box off the back, and walking down towards the deli. It seems the man only took the photo by mistake. He was actually trying to catch a surprise shot of his wife. It seems the courier got in the way." Hermon then showed a couple of shots on the man's cellphone where he'd taken a shot of a woman with her back to the screen and then after the courier, a picture of the woman laughing and facing the screen.

Drummond held out the photos. "Damn. The reporter's doing a better investigation than the police department. That leaves a mark against us. The captain will have our asses when that article hits the streets." Drummond held up the glossy. "What did you find out about the courier company?"

Hermon shrugged. "They have twenty-four-seven service."

Nodding, Drummond dropped his feet to the floor. "Okay, grab your laptop, and let's get over to their office. We need to find the office that box was dropped off at to be delivered."

They spent several hours chasing down a delivery office that could answer their questions. There were thirty of the small drop-off and pick-up offices scattered around the city. Fortunately, they were all tied together on their computer system. The first one the partners went into was able to answer their questions. Without the label, there was no way to find which office had handled the box. Without some type of identity, there was no way to track the particular employee.

Now Hermon and Drummond had to meet with the reporter to see if he'd gotten more information about the courier. Drummond pulled out his cellphone, and using the contact from the reporter, he left a message that they wanted the man to come down to the headquarters the next night for a meeting. They had two more stops by recent sites and some reports to send in as they separated in their different vehicles. They often spent time apart but working together.

By this time, both men called it the end of the work shift. Hermon was off to his beautiful wife. Drummond said he was going to take some time in the warehouse to polish his car and then head home to his cat.

At the beginning of their next night's shift, after filling up on coffee and donuts, the detectives were back at the office.

"There's no reply from the reporter." Hermon was checking their message center through the police system.

"We can call over at the newspaper. They probably have someone on the desk all of the time. What else do you have?" Drummond was pulling papers from one of the printers.

Pointing at a screen, Hermon nodded. "We have that message from the guys over at Station Five about cats."

"What do your computers say about that cop?"

Flying fingers flew over the keys as Drummond opened his coffee to get a smell of the brew. It helped get rid of the office's odor full of small printers and loads of files and paper. While he waited, he sent off a message to Sarah, thinking of the beautiful woman who also loved cats and other animals.

I would love to bring you a latte later tonight. D.

Drummond was surprised he got a message back immediately.

D. Glad to have the latte. I have a strange problem. The hospital has had a request for an offer from someone who wants to purchase all of the cats involved with the crime scenes, including the one found at the deli bombing. I returned that they were not up for adoption yet. Then we got a return from an attorney who said these cats needed to be returned to their owner immediately. S.

By this time, Smitty had brought up the usual ID's of Ronson and his partner Forrest. These two were in their fifties and had a good long record. Forrest was an African American, and Ronson was from the Bronx, New York. That made them an unusual pair, but Drummond and Smith were also an unusual pair, and sometimes opposites worked better together. They filled in the cracks for each other. The two detectives at Station Five had a good record and seemed to be streetwise.

Drummond looked at the clock and decided to call Ronson. He got the standard *leave a message* so the man was busy or eating with his family or had gone to bed early.

"What is it they're working on that might have to do with cats?" Drummond waited while Hermon worked and brought up a report on one of the screens.

These older detectives were good. They'd filed all the records about the unusual suicide with the gun that had gone off twice. It had the location and a description of the room and the gun.

"I don't see it, partner. What do cats have to do with this case for these two detectives?" Hermon was now looking at pictures of the actual body in that high office.

"You know, while you look at pictures, I think I'll go over to that scene and look at it with my own eyes. Maybe there are a lot of cat hairs on the scene that those guys are waiting for forensics to put in their reports." Drummond grabbed his phone and his long leather jacket. "I might pick up some coffee and a latte for a friend while I'm out."

"No problem, keep in contact." As usual, the two partners often worked apart but still close together.

CHAPTER ELEVEN

The tall office building had its parking area underneath. It was easy to pull into off of the main wide avenue. It was well-lit, and that late at night, still had quite a few cars parked near the elevator and stair entries. There were three entries for such a large tall building, one in the middle and two at either end. The cars gathered like flies around dead food at these places, and Drummond brought the *Charger* over near an exit. He decided it might be better to get out of here in a hurry as he walked over to the elevator to go up to the almost top floor.

The elevator's doors opened at one end of a long hallway. The entire area was well-lit. On one side were open doors to offices that probably looked to the outside. On the other side was a large room that was lost in darkness. It was obviously a bunch of divided cubbyhole workstations, empty at this time.

The hair on the back of Drummond's neck stood up as he hesitated when the elevator doors closed behind him. He fisted his hands and felt the large ring on his right hand. It was platinum and looked like the skeleton head of a ram with large horns wrapped around, and as they made their final turn, they continued around his finger. It was big and drew a lot of attention.

At the other end of the hall was the door to the office of the crime scene. The yellow police ribbon was broken. As he stood solid on both feet, planted as if for a fight, a figure appeared in the door. It was just a large black outline due to the lit windows behind it. The sheet of the occult flowed down the hallway and hit Drummond like a wind down on the open streets. Except here it was his inner warnings that were ruffled, not his coat blown back like in a heavy breeze.

The shadow stepped out into the light of the hallway, and Drummond felt more than a breeze — he felt a hurricane. This male was strong and wicked. Under different conditions, there would've been lightning flashing between them down the hallway. It seemed the male was also frozen in place for a moment, as the only thing that moved was a grey cat that escaped from the room. It ran past his legs and between the darkness of the nearest desk to disappear down into the large work area.

The temperature had dropped several degrees, and there was a creak from the ceiling. Could conjuring bring down a building of this size? At last, the man dressed in the obviously custom-made brown suit spoke. "There's a conference room halfway down on the outside. Two doors. You enter your end, and I'll enter from mine. We can talk there in privacy, away from the cameras." He nodded up at the standard round fixtures on the upper walls.

Drummond shrugged, and then, as the man began to move, he also walked down the cold hall to the indicated open door. Once they both stepped in, the hall seemed to change and brighten. The man walked to the end of a long, oblong conference table to move the chair so he could sit down. Drummond sat down at the opposite end but put his large metal ring on the table to protect him from all the wood.

The man put his hand on the table, and the windows began to frost up on the inside. This man in the fancy brown suit also had a large ring on his hand, and it was really interesting. It was a wide round ring that covered the entire area from the knuckle down. It was on the left hand and the third finger like a wedding ring.

Most people would find it an odd, unusual ring like the

ram's head ring that Drummond wore. The inside portion was titanium, and wrapped around it was a design that had dark wood strips on each outside, next to narrow thin strips of light wood, and in the middle, a nice wide strip that was made from what looked like deer antler. The antler was laid down smoothly, and all were polished with patterns that could be seen in the wood and antler. It was a wedding ring for a wood witch—who was married to his magic. It was an evil marriage that involved Satan as the cleric.

"What're you doing in my enclave, wizard?" The man's voice carried around the room like its own shadow.

Drummond made a great show of looking around and then stared directly into the man's dark brown eyes. "Strange, I thought this was the offices of Bildof Investments."

Now the man showed a small evil smile. "I don't think someone with your talents is here for investment in bonds."

Leaving his left hand on the table with the ring to protect him, he reached into his pocket with the right and put more protection on the table. It was the gold shield of a city detective.

Now there was a firmer tone that seemed more normal in the man as he spoke. "Well, well. What has the city gone and done? Started a new cult?"

Without moving or allowing his voice to change in tone, Drummond made a point to stare at the man. "The city fights crime in whatever form the crime comes in. What did you have to do with the unusual suicide of Mr. Connors?"

"Hmm. Suicide. Yes, poor Pierce, he was so despondent for the last week. His job had a lot of demands, and it didn't seem he was up to meeting the deadlines. The bosses upstairs were looking at replacing him. Yes, poor Pierce." The man tapped his wooden ring on the wooden table.

In response, Drummond tapped his heavy ring on the table. There was no response, and as he listened, there was no noise from outside the room. "You're working here alone to-night. But you crossed the police line. That's prohibited. Why?"

"Oh, I chased a cat out of the room. Those feral cats are everywhere in this city." The man, at last, raised his ringed hand and waved it as a gesture.

"What's your name for the record?" Drummond now moved his hand and pulled out the usual small notepad and pen.

"Oh, yes. How rude of me. I'm Elroy Wilmor. I'm also a Senior Executive for Bildof Investments. I work down the hall." The man also waved his hand as if to indicate another room.

Nodding, Drummond wrote. "And where were you when the accident occurred?"

"I was talking to his aide at her desk right outside his office and heard the noise. The girl screamed, and I went in. I saw him and the blood, and she came in after me. Of course, I pulled her out and told her to call the police. I went over to check for a pulse and found out he was dead. I left the room." Again, he raised his hand and waved.

The room had settled down with the temperature coming down to normal. The frost on the window was disappearing. Drummond felt the issue was over. The wood witch had tested him, and finding no cracks in his wall, he withdrew. That didn't mean the war was over, just that there was a respite.

Standing up, Drummond put his notepad away and picked up his badge. "I think that's all. Put the ribbon back up and keep everyone out until the police say the room is clear."

The wood witch stood up with a smile, but he didn't walk closer or offer a hand. No, there would be no touching. "I hope the room will be released soon, as I've been promoted, and that will be my office."

Looking at the man in the brown suit, Drummond noticed he was almost as tall as Drummond, but slimmer. Still, he believed the man was powerful. He just nodded without any comment and went out of the room to go to the end of the hall. His senses told him that Elroy didn't come out of the conference room without having to look back. Drummond decided to take the stairs for a couple of floors. From there, he walked through the dimly lit offices to a different elevator down to the fifth floor. There, he took the stairs to the parking garage.

It might've been a long trip that wasn't necessary, as perhaps the wood witch hadn't tried to put him in danger as he left the building. Still, it was better to be safe than taking chances. Walking slowly around to get to his car, he checked his phone for messages and sent another one to Sarah. He smiled since thinking of her brought heat to his groin. He also sent a message to Hermon to let him know he was coming back to the office.

The purr of the *Hellcat* engine was reflected from the low cement roof of the parking garage. He pulled out and was still in reverse when, in the dim aisle, a large black SUV turned the corner above too fast. It had its bright lights on, and the glare was in his eyes, and the car bore down on him with no intent to stop. The front of the car had one of those large push bumpers that were metal bars that covered up almost over the front of the hood. It was obvious the thing was built for heavy damage, and it was aimed right at him. Without hesitation, he put his arm up on the back of the passenger seat and tromped on the gas to let those thick back wheels pull him down the slope of the parking lot.

The low-built heavy *Charger* made it to the first U-turn and was holding to the pavement as Drummond pulled the wheel without letting up on the fuel. He heard the SUV squeal as it also made an effort to pull through the turn. He was putting distance between them as he got to the next turn, leading to an exit. The SUV scraped something coming out of the turn, and then it was in a straight run that allowed the driver to take advantage of weight and the downhill slope.

Flipping down the sun shield to get the bright lights out of his face, Drummond slammed through the next turn and then made a change of the wheel as he headed for the exit. Except it was an entrance, but fortunately, at this late at night, it was empty.

As he made it out onto the upgrade to the street, he heard the thunder of the crash as the big car didn't make the final turn. As for Drummond, he slammed the car into first gear as soon as the back wheels hit the street and handled expertly as the car did a small buck. He pulled over to the curb and pulled out the mic. "Code nine at"—he looked out to find an address—"one-two-four-four Midway, Parking garage." Code 9 was a standard notice for all police that said a cop needed assistance immediately.

Drummond got out of the car, put a sign in the window, and his badge on his jacket collar. He pulled his *Glock* and moved close to the entrance to wait a minute to see if anyone was coming out. He heard a siren in the distance, but even better, an unmarked car pulled up with its light in the front window. Two police dressed in civilian clothes jumped out.

"You okay?" one officer asked.

"I'm fine. A big SUV tried to take me out, and it crashed inside. No shots fired."

The guy who spoke immediately took a position at the other side of the entrance.

The other guy started running as he yelled, "I'll cover the next entrance."

By the time Drummond and the other officer began to enter, a standard black and white pulled up and killed its siren, and a guy in blue jumped out. Drummond brought him up to date over the mic as he moved into the low-ceiling garage.

There was the sound of a gunshot down toward the other exit.

"Go help your partner. I'll check the car and get your six." Drummond hollered as he ran toward the wreck. The other cop took off.

Drummond worked toward the big car that was slammed into the rear end of an equally large van. The marriage didn't work for either, as the wall in front of the van objected to the interference of the van's bumper. The SUV was deeply into the back of the unprotected rear of the van. With some metal being flung, the few lights in this area were out, and seeing into the SUV was impossible from a distance.

Easing up on the damaged car with his gun in front, Drummond, at last had a view into the front seat through the tinted broken glass. There was a body slumped over the deflated protective airbag into the steering wheel. There was no way to get the bent door open, but Drummond reached in and felt for a pulse in the neck. No, this guy was beyond saving. Pulling out a small pen flashlight, Drummond checked the rest of the car, and it was empty. The passenger door was open.

Now, he turned and ran after the other cop to see if they could catch the runaway passenger. They had him. The man was down on the cement, bleeding out. By the time Drummond got there, the man was surrounded by a flock of cops. Drummond gave information about the dead man in the SUV and gave his card to several men. He would send a copy of his report to their captains, and then he was out, heading for the office.

He needed his partner's smiling face and some calm. What the hell could go wrong?

CHAPTER TWELVE

So much for calm and rest — their captain met him as he came up to the top of the steps. He told Drummond to pick up his partner to check on a missing reporter at the city newspaper.

"We need to go over past the main office of the newspaper." Hermon was shutting down all the computers.

"No problem. We can go there and then head on home since our shift is done. I want to tell you about my trip downtown. I've found our murderer, and there's no way of proving he did anything." Drummond never had a chance to sit down in his side of the office.

The partners made the decision to stop off at the newspaper reporter's apartment on their way home in the early morning hours. When they got to the reporter's home, the site was already under control by the local station. They ducked under the yellow tape and entered the apartment with their gold shields pinned on their collars. The first fact was that the apartment had been ransacked. Everything had been opened and thrown out on the floor or furniture.

Okay, someone was looking for information that Milligan had, and they thought it might be in his home. Except Drummond thought they didn't find it, or they would've stopped. With his height, he leaned and saw into the bedroom, which was also a mess. He would guess the bathroom was torn apart to match everything else.

A CSI in civilian clothes stepped forward. "Good morning, detectives. We've already checked for the standard traces."

She pointed at what they'd added to the destroyed rooms. Dusted black fingerprint material was everywhere. A second guy was picking up the yellow numbered locators used for the pictures and collections of important traces.

She smiled as she waved her hand. "You can walk through, but please don't move anything."

"No problem, we just want to take a look." Hermon took out his *iPad* and began taking pictures. Drummond and he both agreed ages ago that he could get better shots with the larger unit.

Drummond turned to the CSI gal and stopped her. "So, with all of this mess, did you find any trace of Milligan being killed or hurt? Any trace of his blood?"

"No blood." She shook her head. "In fact, the lack of fingerprints and human traces is disturbing."

Nodding, Drummond leaned against the wall and watched Hermon work the rooms without stumbling too much. "You've told me what you didn't find. Can you tell me what did you find?"

"Oh, you're going to love this. Broken antique pottery and cat hair." The gal was grinning, seeming to wait for him to ask the right question.

Playing the game, Drummond smiled with a lift on one side of his mouth and went ahead and did what the lady wanted. "Okay, with this mess, why are those two items important?"

"With all the shamble in this apartment, even in the kitchen and the bathroom, the only things that got broken are two antique statues." She shrugged and nodded at a sealed box that was sitting in the middle of the floor. "We'll get a better look at them when we have them back at the lab."

"And the cat?" Drummond encouraged the CSI gal.

"The cops checked all the neighbors, and they said he didn't have a pet. There's no cat food in the kitchen, and no bowls on the floor to provide for a pet. But there are traces of a calico cat on everything. It's like the poor thing was scared and was running over all the furniture to get away."

Drummond couldn't resist letting the CSI lady have fun. "Did you find the kitty?"

"Nope, it just left us the hairs before it disappeared, as the first person from the newspaper opened the door." She nodded, and he knew she meant a man who they'd seen in the lobby.

Shaking his head, Drummond thought about furry cats. That brought to mind the smooth skin under the breast of a beautiful cat lover, and he pulled out his phone. There was no message from Sarah. He sent out a burst.

Sarah. I know you're busy, but I'd love to share coffee and a moment of . . . .

He pushed send and looked up to see if Hermon was about done tripping over his own feet. "Partner, I'm going down to the lobby."

"Okay," Hermon mumbled as he headed into the bathroom.

Going back down to the lobby, Drummond found two street police officers in blue talking to a civilian. They stepped back and nodded as he approached.

"Are you the person from the newspaper that opened Milligan's apartment?" he asked as he accepted the driver's license from one of the cops. The youngster had a reporter's ID on a long ribbon around his neck. It was the standard one issued to the news companies by the police department. They were handed out with ease and without any questions.

"Yep, the boss was mad because Roger Milligan had missed two deadlines. He pulled me out and sent me over here. Thought that Milligan was drunk and needed a wake-up call since he wasn't answering any of his phones." The kid just talked as if he didn't believe in sentences, running his words all together and fast.

"Has Mr. Milligan missed deadlines in the past?" Drummond handed the license back to the policeman.

"Actually, no, the guy's like a computer himself, and he's always pounding out words on time or before the editor yells. I want to be like him."

"Well, who knows, maybe you will when you grow up." Drummond walked away and looked out at the sun coming up and thought about the missing sleep. He also thought about another cat that was waiting at home that needed the litter box cleaned.

At about that time, Hermon came down, hopping sideways on the last step to catch himself on the railing. Drummond shook his head, but in all the time they'd worked together, Drummond never reached out to help his inept partner. He would never draw attention to the brilliant man's strange way of handling his skinny, awkward body.

The nice part about having a computer nerd partner was that he'd file their reports while Drummond drove them home. Most of the so-called paperwork would be waiting on their captain's desk when the next night's shift started. That meant it was on the computer for the main man and was printing out on a unit near an aide who stapled and filed.

CHAPTER THIRTEEN

Anger was not the correct word that Elroy felt as he headed out of the city, having the sun rising in his rearview mirror. Who would have thought that a detective in this forsaken city would be a wizard? No, not a wizard, a rare master wizard.

Now, he was heading out to seek advice from a hated wood coven. Not that they could hurt him. No, his pain was all in his past. The pain was what had made him.

He'd lived with his mother in a small neighborhood on the edge of the city. At six, he went to his first kindergarten class, and that was when he found out most of the kids had fathers. He asked Mom where his daddy was, and she said that Daddy was away and it wouldn't be good when Daddy came home. She told him to forget about Daddy and not mention him again. Her frown was the meanest he'd seen, so he obeyed.

For the first ten years of his life, he was a normal little boy with friends, schoolwork, and a bike. His friends played out in the rain, and there was tag, ballgames, and lots of fun. He was sitting at the kitchen table, eating a peanut butter and strawberry jelly sandwich. That was his favorite lunch, which Mom had surprised him with when she called him inside.

Next week was his eleventh birthday, and he was hoping for a nice big chocolate cake. Maybe Mom would even be able to afford that new mitt he'd seen in the window down at the sports store. That was the day he first met his father. The man came in through the front door without knocking or without saying anything. Mom had stood up to see who was there. She then stood back to lean against the cabinet, as the tall man came into the kitchen, pulled out a chair, and sat at the table.

The man spoke in a voice that made Elroy quit eating his favorite food. "He has a birthday coming up?"

Behind Elroy, he heard his mother whimpering. "Yes, sire."

"Was he not to be sent to me, his father, at age ten?" The harsh voice demanded.

Now Elroy's eyes were really wide, and he was breathing in short gasps. Had he heard, right? Was this tall scary-looking man with the dark brown-streaked eyes really his father? The mean man was so tall and looked like a killer from the movies on TV.

"Elroy, go to your room." It was his mother with her hands on his shoulders. Later, he would realize it was the last words she'd spoken to him.

It was from his room that the big man had taken him, lifting him from the floor to pull him from the house and throw him in through the open window of the back seat of a car. Elroy was confused, crying, and hurt. But none of it was near the pain he would feel in the following few years. There were two days and nights of traveling. They ate in the car, and he had to do his business on the side of the road with some paper to wipe with. They finally stopped deep in some type of forest that didn't seem like the parks he'd visited.

There were people here around a campfire, but it wasn't a happy group like he expected. There was no fun food and games for the other boys that he saw, all huddled around in the flickering dark. Someone hollered at Elroy's father, and they all settled down and ignored the kids. Elroy made his way slowly over to the other boys. The kids all looked frightened, and Elroy felt the same. What was this all about? Elroy wanted to go home.

After the adults ate, they gave the boys some sandwiches along with one bottle of water. But they weren't given blankets, and then they all finally fell asleep, too tired to fight the darkness. Elroy was one of the last to sleep, since he was as much excited as frightened.

He had his hand wrapped around the half-full bottle of water. In the flickering light, he could read the brand, *Deer Park*, but what was better was the brown figure of a deer's head. He looked over at the bottles near him. He reached out to pull a full one over and tucked it into his jacket. Elroy was saving it just because of the picture.

Morning came almost before the sun had got up enough to bring light into the forest. In the dim fog, they were woken with a lot of noise and the smell of cooking. But as the seven boys stirred, suddenly, in the dim fog, they were grabbed by their thin arms and pulled upward. An older woman was yelling at them. "If you're hungry, remember it. If you're thirsty, remember it. It's all here, and all you have to do is let the trees help you find your way back here. Become part of the wood."

Elroy didn't resist as a dirty bag covered his head. He was lifted to be placed on something flat next to another boy who was crying. He was listening, hoping to hear the voice of the man who claimed to be his father. What he heard was that old woman giving orders. "If they try to pull off the hoods, tie their hands. Let's get going."

Elroy didn't want his hands tied, so he sat quietly, not touching his hood. Then, what they were sitting on began to move. It seemed to be a wagon pulled by a small vehicle. He knew from watching TV and the big kids in the neighborhood that an ATV was probably pulling it. That was cool. He felt some of the boys trying to move around, and a couple were crying. Elroy just sat silently, listening. He decided he didn't like this man who claimed to be his father. He didn't like that old woman who gave orders. He wanted to be home with his mom and his old ball mitt. He'd get through the woods with the help of trees and get to the food.

The ride was rough as they bounced against the wood of the flat wagon. He had no idea how long the ride was, but it seemed forever. When it stopped, they were pulled from the surface and dumped on the ground. Now their hoods were removed. Looking around, Elroy saw nothing but a deep, tangled, untamed forest with a full sun making streams straight down through a few breaks in the tall, heavy trees. In between, the thick trunks were bushes, most with thorns and pointed leaves.

Sitting or standing, the boys looked at each other and around. Then the adults were on the wagon and the motor vehicle began to move and were soon gone without a word. The adults continued moving forward from the direction they had come, breaking bushes as they moved back and forth among the tree trunks.

"I'm hungry." Once one of the boys said the words, it was a disease that spread. Everyone's stomach felt empty.

"I need a drink," another boy whined. Now a couple began to cry.

Two of boys turned and began to follow the crushed path of the disappeared wagon ahead. By this time, they couldn't even hear the sound of the motor. But the debris of broken limbs left a clear trail.

But another boy started on the path from the direction that they'd come from, the same amount of broken shrubs and torn limbs leaving a path. That left four of them undecided. One boy just sat down on the ground, crying and muttering. But Elroy ignored them all and thought about the hated man who had taken him away from the warm house with the hot meals.

What had he and the woman said? Was this a game? Become part of the wood. What did that mean? Elroy knew he had the strange, brown-streaked eyes just like the mean man. Did they look like the wood in the center of trees? He looked at the others who were still near, and they also had that strange color to their eyes. Were they all some type of special boys? Without saying anything, he turned off the path and walked into a bright spot of sunlight. It was just a small stream that came down through the leaves of a giant tree, like the one across the street from his house.

He went over through the prickly bushes and put his hand on the wide trunk. He tried to forget the mean man, as he wanted to remember what he'd learned in school. He enjoyed what was taught in grade school biology classes. So, moss grew on the north side of the tree. He felt around the big trunk and down low and found the soft growth. Now he wouldn't walk in circles. What direction was the food located in? He wasn't going to cry, but he had no idea. A couple of the boys were standing on the track, watching him.

As he stood, the sun had moved a fraction, and the stream of sunlight had shifted on the floor to highlight some flowers and berries on the bottom of some bushes.

"Hey, can we eat those?" One of the boys walked closer.

Elroy looked down and noticed that some of the berries were drying up on the stems. "I don't think so. If the birds didn't eat any before they're drying up, they must be poison."

"Oh, yeah. Smart. Wait until we find something that the animals are eating." The other boy tried to sound smart, but his voice broke with some fear.

Elroy tried hard to remember the school lessons. With that short movement of shadow from the sun, wait, it meant he now had east and west. In the camp when the sun was barely coming up, it was coming up in the east.

"I know the way to the camp and food." He announced proudly. His problem meant that he couldn't take the easy route on the path trampled by wagon. He would have to walk through the tough underbrush. Also, it would be a long walk. Walking in the forest was hard work, but Elroy wasn't going to cry anymore. He was going to get to the camp, and then he was going to get home to his mom. He would learn, and maybe he would hit the big mean one who claimed to be his father. He would find food, and he would learn.

After getting into thorns, Elroy learned to take the long way around the bushes with the shiny leaves. It wasn't long before he knew that at least one other boy was following him. That was okay, but he kept his hidden water bottle a secret. Walking around big trees and the sharp bushes, Elroy was getting tired and thirsty. At last, he tripped over a limb he didn't see on the ground, and when he went down, he stayed beside the wood from the tree above.

It was about his ball bat's size at home, and he just kept his hand on it, as it seemed to give him comfort. Now, there was one boy close and another behind him.

As Elroy had tripped, the heavy bottle of water had fallen out of his pocket.

"Oh, you have water. Good, my name is Milton. Can I have a drink?" Milton reached out his hand, but Elroy had quickly retrieved his precious water. Elroy just shook his head and held the bottle close to his body.

Milton stood and looked at Elroy for a moment, but then he smiled. He reached into his pocket, pulled out a long brown item, and raised it to let Elroy see what was in his hand. "I have a candy bar. We can share. I'll give you some of my candy for some of your water."

Rising, Elroy looked beyond Milton at the other boy, who was smaller but had a strange rat-like look to his face. "Hey, guys. I want some, too."

Milton turned and looked at the other boy who was approaching. "Well, what do you have to eat?"

"Nothing." The boy looked at both of them with a frown. "But I have a knife." He was holding out a type of knife that folded, but it now was open. Elroy thought it looked long and frightening. "I can cut the candy bar into pieces for all of us."

"I don't think so." Milton held his precious candy bar behind him and stood his ground. Before anything else was said, there was a fight. Both boys were on the ground, wrestling in the odd way that young children did, with funny punches.

There was a screech, and then Milton was partway up with the knife in his hand, and the other kid wasn't doing anything. Elroy stood with the limb in his hand.

Later, he didn't remember why he'd swung the limb, but he did remember the saying. *Become part of the wood.* The limb connected solidly with the back of Milton's head, and he was down next to the other kid, and it was suddenly silent in the forest. It was dark where they were, but Elroy could see a shaft of sunlight in the distance.

With no thought, he moved over and picked up the candy bar and then also reached out to pick up the knife. He wiped the wetness off on the leaves on the ground. He didn't want to wait to see if either boy got up to ask for shares, so he began to walk in what he thought was the right direction. He tucked his new treasures into his pockets and kept the limb with him. *Become part of the wood.* He liked the limb better than the two boys who'd fought. He took out the knife and figured out how to fold it and put it away. He also pulled out the candy bar and took a big bite before putting it back into a deep pocket.

He walked all day and into the dark of night, eating small bites and taking a sip or two. He stopped to pee and then moved on, refusing to stop to rest. It was in the dark that he finally saw the flickering light of the campfire. He just walked up and sat down near the warmth. He said nothing, and no one spoke to him. But the cranky old woman passed him a plate.

It was full of food, so he decided even though he was tired enough to sleep, the walk through the woods was worth the trek. There were two hotdogs with ketchup, potato salad, and chocolate chip cookies.

Elroy smiled as he thought about chocolate chip cookies. To this day, they were his favorite dessert. But now his anger was still burning inside.

CHAPTER FOURTEEN

The start of another shift brought another complaint from their captain that a missing person's report had been bumped up to Major Case from Missing Persons, because the person was important. Drummond did a double-take when he saw the information on Hermon's screen. The missing person was Dr. Sarah Aggar. Yes, she was important enough to be bumped up to CI.

"Smith, we need to get to her apartment. This is important for me." With that, they were on their way in a reckless drive across the wet streets in the nighttime traffic. This time, Drummond didn't need the directions from Hermon's computer as he pulled up in front of the building that Aggar owned.

There were a few black and white cars and a large unmarked van in front of the sidewalk. The steps going up were set off with the usual yellow tape. With their gold shields clipped to their front lapels, the two partners hurried up the short entry into her home. Inside, there were a lot of police and still a couple of CSI people.

There was also the woman who was the receptionist from the main animal clinic. Drummond didn't know her name, but she immediately turned to walk over to him.

"Oh, thank God, you're here, Detective Drummond. Look what's happened in here. Look at her pets, Midnight and Cayo." The woman went over to the dog that was lying on the floor. It was still alive, but it had injuries. The fat cat was now twice its size, and it was no longer inactive as it stood near the

79

dog. It was standing with its tail straight out and its full protective mode as if it'd been struck by lightning, but it was anger that caused that attitude.

"Poor Cayo needs help, and Midnight the cat won't let us near him. The cat still has claws and teeth even though she's old." As another young man entered carrying a travel pet cage and a small, strange-looking pistol, the woman waved a hand.

"What's that?" Drummond asked as he watched the CSI guys in the bedroom.

"We might have to shoot her with a tranq." The woman sounded very sad. "I know that Doc Sarah would hate that."

Looking back at the cat that was ready to attack anyone who came near the injured dog, Drummond held up his hand. "Let me try something. Give me a treat for both animals."

Waiting for a moment as the woman hunted and then gave him a small bit of the end of a soft bone treat and then a smaller round bit that he knew his own cat, also called Midnight, would appreciate. Now he checked his big ring and then slipped out of his long leather jacket. He walked slowly towards the animals, but not directly, stopping beside the cat that was hissing. He just stood quietly for a few seconds before he went down on a knee. He held his hand out flat with the two treats in front of the angry cat and waited.

After a moment, waiting to see if the cat was going to bite him or take the treat, Midnight huffed, and her fur began to settle, and she gently lapped up the cat treat. Drummond laid the piece of dog treat in front of the dog's nose, and it did move. At last, a dry tongue came out, and the treat was gone without much movement. Drummond reached out and put the large hand with the ring on it under the cat's fat belly and picked her up slowly. She finally leaned against his chest as he stood. Her purr was deep as she closed her eyes.

The young man sat down the carry case and the odd gun

and came forward to reach out to the nose of the injured dog. He was smart and let the dog smell for a second before he ran his hand down the flank of the three-legged injured dog.

Turning, Drummond handed off the cat to the woman and ignored the room. He walked to the door of the bedroom. He knew he couldn't enter because the covered CSI team was working, and it was a mess. Things hadn't just been gone through—they were destroyed. Dresser drawers were in pieces, hardly recognizable. Clothes weren't just thrown out across the room—they were torn into pieces that would never be put together ever again. The windows were broken outward, and the rods were drooping with no drapes to be seen, probably part of the torn items throughout the area.

What the CSI people were doing, without disturbing anything, was taking pictures first. A guy with a blue disposable suit and booties on came over to the door, being very careful where he stepped.

He nodded. "Detective. We'll spray luminol for blood traces next before we move anything. There's no obvious blood signs and no marks on the walls or doors that we can see without moving anything."

Now Drummond left the home to go back out to the wet streets and get fresh air. The team had two missing person cases, one that was important to the city and one that was important to Drummond. Leaning against his car, he hunted out a wooden match and put the dead-end into his mouth. He had a double problem, and he needed the brilliant mind of his partner. He felt that he knew who was behind all the deaths at the different spas.

But worse, that dangerous person was probably behind the reporter and the vet being missing. The nosy reporter had probably come across something that led him to the wood witch. As for Sarah, her love for animals, especially cats, and the fact that she'd kept the ones connected with the crimes segregated meant that she also must've come across some-thing that she wanted to tell Drummond.

Now the wood witch had taken these two people, and he was too clever to kill them and leave them somewhere to be identified or tied to him. For Drummond and for their lives, time was not on their side. There were things he could do on his magic side, but for the police department and the city, there had to be tangible proof. It had to be there, or else the reporter and Sarah wouldn't be missing. Now, all he had to do was find it. That meant they had to trace the two missing people backward to the exact point where they were taken.

There was also the fact that he had to convince his partner that they had to investigate Elroy Wilmor, a very rich and im-portant man. Convincing his partner, Hermon Smith, was the easy part. As a team for several years and having saved each other in some serious situations, what one wanted the other would agree to and go along as needed.

Now sitting together in the car, Drummond explained that he'd met with Mr. Wilmor at the office. He explained that the man had acted strangely. "He's connected or behind the deaths at the different places all around the town where street beggars were killed. We're going to have a hard time proving it because he's extremely smart." Drummond was wrapping up his appeal to his partner.

"Okay, no problem. We can do a background check on the big shot. I can do that deeper than anyone else in this city." Hermon was working the small but special computer on his skinny knees with the car seat pushed back.

"Right, and we'll head back to the newspaper office. We need to trace what the reporter was checking on. Then where he drank his coffee in the morning and his whiskey at night." With that, Drummond had the muscle car in gear, heading to the offices that were open all day and night.

The newspaper offices were like the police department.

Items for print happened at all times of the day and night. They might have special hours for the large presses to run, but the workers were on duty at odd hours with different people hired for the work at unusual time periods. As for the reporters and the people who supported them, they worked at any time that the news needed to be covered, put into computers or photographs.

The official front office and big doors were locked, but the side doors and the parking areas were busy and open. A chief editor was on duty for all three shifts, so the one on duty, as the two detectives entered the offices, wasn't happy. There was something different about this news building. It was new, but inside, it smelled old. Each floor was almost the same, large open spaces full of desks, free-standing cabinets, and baskets with lots of things blocking the aisles.

There were dark offices at the end of the large rooms, and there were tall dirty windows with many posters, signs, and notes or letters pasted on them on either side. Even the empty desks looked busy and cramped. They were full of open folders and computer screens with something floating on them. The chairs had long become a mismatch of private choice, some standard office desk chairs on rollers. Many straight-back chairs were by desks and in the spaces that were in the way as one walked toward an office.

The smell here was of dust, paper, and ink, along with old uneaten lunches. Up by the walls as high as one could reach were stacks of boxes, and above them were dusty marks from unknown sources. The surprise was that the long streams of overhead lights were all on, and every single one was lit and bright. Someone might not keep the place clean on the floor, but they took care of the bulbs in those florescent receptacles above. Whoever paid the electric bill was keeping the City Electric Company happy.

They needed the fifth floor, which was at the top of this

building. The presses and printing were done in an attached structure just as tall. There were a couple of open elevators, but the two detectives chose to walk up the main wide stairs. This allowed them to take a moment on each floor to catch Hermon's breath and look the whole business over.

CHAPTER FIFTEEN

Drummond headed to where reporter Roger Milligan's working place was in the back. It was near where the dark offices were located. That was also were the editor for this shift was in his office, ranting loudly. He was heard yelling into a phone.

This called for the big girth of Drummond, with both of them wearing their gold shields on the low sides of their front collars. As the big guy, he led the way to the open door of the place where they knew they would get little information. They did have a nice blue folded paper to allow them to look at Milligan's desk. The pretty blue paper was official and had been signed by a judge.

Of course, the whole conversation went as expected. The man yelled at them, but Drummond yelled louder. The editor swore that he was going to throw them out, saying something about laws to protect the news. Drummond gave him the pretty blue folded form. As the editor turned red, the phone rang, and Drummond turned Hermon to go to the correct desk.

They began to search through drawers and the computer. Hermon took out a thumb drive and put it into the front of the tower computer, which was sitting on a short cabinet beside the desk. With a few quick strokes on the keyboard, he had the system up and running. They'd already talked about what they would do when inside. And Hermon wouldn't waste time looking at anything now. He'd copy the full memory and look through the files later when he might have to break some passwords.

Drummond was tearing off the top empty sheets of any pads and opened the top drawer, trying not to disturb his partner. The drawer was full of broken pencils, matchbooks from bars, and torn ticket stubs.

At this time, a man in shirtsleeves came down another cluttered aisle to take a seat at the next desk. He didn't even pretend to be busy. He just leaned back in the rolling chair so he could watch them.

"So, is Roger in trouble? Is there a story in it?" The guy smiled as he picked up a small recorder and held it up near his shoulder.

"Isn't he missing?" asked Drummond. "I think that's what his girlfriend said."

"Oh." The reporter put down the recorder. "You already talked to Doris. She has a mouth like a radio, except you can't turn it off."

Giving the reporter his crooked smile, Drummond nodded. "Of course we talked to Doris and several others."

"Yep, I saw you come up through the stairs. You stopped off on the floor for Research, and of course, Doris led you to others. Well, I'm not sharing anything else." With that, the guy pocketed his little recorder and got up. He soon disappeared down the aisle, not speaking to anyone.

Looking at his partner, Drummond shook his head. "Hermon, what floor is Research on?"

Checking something on the computer screen, his nerdy partner smiled. "Hmm, wait a sec. Oh, here it is . . . the second floor."

"Great, that's our next stop."

It only took Hermon a couple of more minutes to get everything off the computer. At the same time, Drummond looked around, getting ideas and watching who was paying attention. The editor ignored them since he had serious problems and was back to yelling on the phone. Guessing that with all the yelling, Drummond thought most of the rest of the big room workers were finding excuses to stay out of sight. At last, Hermon pulled out the thumb drive, did something to the computer to hide where he'd been in the system, and they were ready to retreat.

"This place stinks. I don't know how anyone can work here." Hermon moved around an overflowing trashcan that was out at the end of a desk in the aisle. He stumbled over a box, caught himself on a short cabinet, then knocked folders off onto the floor. He stopped to pick up the papers and folders, but Drummond reached down and grabbed his arm.

"Don't worry. They probably didn't need those anyway." Taking a strong but gentle hold on his partner as he spoke. Drummond pulled Hermon forward around all the things waiting to trip him until they reached the landing before the wide stairs.

On the second floor, about halfway down the room, was a strange set-up. There were large dark screens with people sitting in front of them, mostly younger women. The screens were full of dark grey backgrounds with white lettering or reversed negative photos. Recognizing it, he was surprised that these units were still used with all of the available stuff on the Internet.

Hermon pointed out what they were seeing. "Partner, these are research units. There are large tapes like a movie screen tape on rolls. Evidently, the people here are looking back through old files, probably checking for facts or additional info for articles."

"Okay." Drummond began strolling down aisles that were a little less disarrayed. "Now, we need to find Doris in front of one of those screens."

They got close to the first row of ladies, and the decision was made—should this be a big guy detective or a quiet guy detective? The answer was made when a woman looked up at the two men and just took one look at some very wide shoulders. She began to flutter her eyelids and smiled at Drummond.

"Can I help you . . . I hope?" The woman turned in her chair to cross her legs and let her skirt slide upward.

Giving one of his rare smiles, Drummond tilted his head. "We're looking for Doris."

"Damn, that girl gets all the good ones. You know she has a boyfriend." The woman sighed as she looked over between the large screens at a woman in the next row. It took them a couple of moments to work their way through the separation to the site where Doris was working. Like those around her, she soon looked up as they approached.

Drummond decided to be the tough detective. "Doris, we understand you're a close friend of Roger Milligan?"

"Yes, have you gotten word from him?" The young woman looked up. She looked lovely with brown eyes and a lot of brown and blond streaked hair piled up on her head.

"Let's step out to the stair landing where we can talk, Miss." Drummond helped her up and let her follow Hermon back out of the maze of machines. They then passed the desks to the back of the office space.

"First, we need your full name and address," Drummond spoke, but he stepped back, trying not to intimidate her, letting her see his skinny harmless-looking partner.

Hermon was ready to take down all of the information as they finally relaxed on the large landing.

When Drummond felt she was at ease, he took over. "When was the last time you talked to Mr. Milligan?"

"Oh, he called me to break a date. It wasn't an important date. We get together every Friday for a fish diner at our favorite place. It's Benny's at Fifteenth and Midway Avenue."

"Did he tell you why or where he was going when he

called?" Drummond kept his voice low to encourage her to talk.

"No. We have an understanding. If he's on a story or doing something that he wants to finish, we don't have to make apologies. We'll look forward to the next Friday. He just said he had to follow up on something. He was on the other side of town and wouldn't make our usual date. He also said we would see each other the next day. That would be Saturday."

"And you didn't hear or see him after that last discussion? You know we can check your phone records." Now Drummond used a tougher tone.

"No, sir, I wish I had heard from him. I'm getting worried. This is the longest that we've not talked." The pretty girl looked back and forth between the two of them. "Has something bad happened?"

Now it was up to Hermon. "Now, don't worry. A good reporter like Mr. Milligan can be on something important and doesn't want any interruptions. Here's my card. Call us if you hear from him or hear any information."

With that, the time was getting away from them, so they watched the girl go back to her workspace. They started down the steps with Hermon hanging onto a railing.

"Let's go ahead and put out an APB on our Mr. Milligan," Drummond commented, as he threw out his wooden match. Hermon watched it spiral, catch on fire in mid-air, and then go out as it hit the cement.

"I can do it from the car. Let me open my computer on my lap." Hermon tapped his laptop that was always with him.

"Yep, and please make sure you put your seat belt on tight." With that, Drummond let the *Hellcat* super-charged engine roar as he worried inside about Sarah.

Chapter Sixteen

In a room so black that Sarah couldn't even see her hand when it touched her face, she was trying to move and discover anything. She was able to learn first that she'd been on a metal bed that would move around easily. She could feel the thin mattress on top and nothing more.

As she stood up from the bed, she realized she was still dressed but didn't have any shoes on. The floor felt cold and like metal. Holding out her arms and keeping one leg against the bed, she slid her feet forward. At the end of the frame, there was a metal wall as cold as the one touching her feet.

Following the wall carefully so that she wouldn't fall, her steps were only a short walk with about five or six feet, and there was a corner with another metal wall. Sarah did a light tap on the wall, but it was solid, without any hollow sound.

Now, following the new wall, she just let her hands lead her down a new wall that went on for about fifteen feet with no interruption. What she found was nothing but cold metal and another corner.

Having no choice, she took a deep breath and moved forward, keeping her hands on the wall. Her success was limited. She found what she thought was a door. But there were no hinges and no handle. It must've opened out with the attachments on the other side. On her side, it was all smooth with a fit so tight she couldn't fit her fingers into the lines of the four-foot-wide opening.

Moving on, the last corner took her back to the bed. *Damn,* she knew she was really in trouble, but she didn't know why.

Sarah sat down on the thin mattress to get her feet off the cold floor. She tried to think why someone would kidnap her. Yes, she did have money, but there was no family for them to try to get the funds for her release from. She couldn't think of any secrets or information that she had that might be important enough that someone would need to keep her out of the public. If there was something she did know, why not just kill her? Everything just seemed to be a big question.

Stretching her arms and bending her head to ease her neck, she thought about what was missing in the room. Actually, everything was missing, as there was nothing except the bed, unless there was something small in the middle. Okay, standing up with her arms out in front and palms flat, she slowly slid her feet forward to move across the room.

It was a slow search, but her palms reached the wall before her toes touched anything but the cold, smooth metal floor. Sarah decided while she was here on this wall that she should move around to the place with the door and try to get attention. When she found the outline of the door, she began to pound and yell. She remembered the American Kobby cats that had the loudest voice, and she raised her voice to a higher pitch.

"Hey, help. I need to find a bathroom." Sarah slapped her palms on the door. "I need to take a piss. I don't want to have a urine smell in my room." She pounded with a fist. "Hey."

There was a knock, and down by her feet, a small door swung open. It wasn't large enough for her to crawl through, but it was big enough for the large bucket to be pushed in by a hand covered in a black glove. As the soft light began to shine in, Sarah immediately leaned over, trying to see out to get an idea of where she was and who belonged to the black glove. There was a roll of toilet paper also set on the floor beside the bucket. Unfortunately, the door was closed quickly.

She could hear the voice that someone was disguising as

they spoke. "Leave the bucket there, and I'll empty it."

Hesitating, Sarah decided to answer but tried to stay in some control. "Okay, but give me a moment."

Picking up the bucket, she thought of her many animals back at the hospital and her pets in her home. She took a smell with her head down close to the inside of the pale. It just smelled clean and of an antiseptic. Then she brought the edge of the handle near her nose, and yes, there it was a man's aftershave. It was something that was sold in most stores, a better brand, but not too expensive.

She wasn't sure she remembered the brand's name, but she would know when she smelled it again on a man. Well, with that in mind, she put the bucket down and went ahead and pulled down her panties and used the damn thing. She decided to carefully put the rest of the paper down next to the wall when she was done. She moved the bucket to what she thought was the proper place and worked her way to the bed to lie down and stare up at the darkness.

This was going to drive her crazy. Sarah had to find something to keep her mind busy as she went ahead and lay with her eyes open, seeing nothing. Lying on her back, she finally had an idea. She rolled over and stretched out on the floor. Sarah hoped this would give her a better view out of the small opening when the man came for the bucket. At least she knew that one of her captures was a male and wore special aftershave cologne that she would recognize in the future.

There was no way to tell time, and within the dark, it could have been hours or a few minutes when Sarah heard a noise in the wall next to the bed. It was a thumping sound, as if someone was knocking on the wall. Kneeling on her bed, she placed her ear against the metal wall, and sure enough, there was a thump, thump against that wall. Someone was banging on the other side of it. But what were they hammering with? Sarah had already discovered that her hands and feet wouldn't make a loud sound. Was there another person being held in this dark place? If so, what were they using to make the thuds?

Feeling where her knees were in contact with the thin mattress, Sarah realized she hadn't tried to move the metal cot frame. Sliding off the bunk, she pulled, and it moved easily, so she just slammed it against the wall with a heavy push. It made a loud thud. At her thud, there were suddenly two from the other side. Okay, there was another captive. She bumped her bed twice and waited.

The problem was that they didn't have a way of communicating other than a couple of thuds. Sarah didn't know Morse code except for the standard SOS that everyone knew and played with as kids. In the dark, for what she guessed were hours, she and the other prisoner would thump to let each other know there was company. Who was the other person behind the next thick wall?

Time was hard to endure, especially with all the displays around a person. Everywhere Drummond looked was something that gave him the time — it was the way of the world now. There was even a clock in the dashboard of the *Charger*.

When he turned onto the avenue, the big old building, which held the police headquarters, had a clock up high with hands and a light on it to be seen for blocks in this city. His cell phone instantly announced the time in large letters with the day, the month, and date below in smaller letters. Going up the stairs, there was one of the square reflective clocks that did the same thing with big square letters for the time and small ones for all the rest. There was a large round clock on the wall of the big open office space when he entered and worked his way over to the special side office that he and his partner were allowed to use. As soon as he entered the smaller room, nodding to his partner, there was the time in the upper corners of all the screens that were bright in color.

Drummond hated that this reminded him that time was passing, and he wasn't reaching Sarah. With a great amount of energy, he cleared everything off the long back table, piling the boxes and files on the floor. Some items went under the table, and others were in stacks in the corner or on top of the two tall filing cabinets they didn't use.

"Everything okay, buddy?" Hermon slid sideways on his special chair that supported his back as he sat before all the screens.

"No." The word was a harsh grunt from Drummond as he began to search through what he'd taken off the table and put a few things back. "We need to concentrate on certain problems."

"Okay, which ones?" Hermon sounded like he was ready to help. It was how they both worked.

Now Drummond had a large stack on one end and a couple of smaller stacks, and between them was an empty space.

"Hermon, I need labels." He pulled out some more files and had a new stack.

"Give me the names, and I'll print them out faster than you can find the stock." Hermon clicked on some keys.

Pulling out a couple of more folders, Drummond stood up and looked at his partner. "Okay, I need one for each of the following . . . *Bombing, Reporter, Vet,* and *Wood Witch.*"

"They're coming out on the small printer. What's the empty spot for?" Hermon was turning to look at the piles on the table. The pile for the bomb at the deli was large, with so many interviews and copies of vids included.

Pointing at the vacant spot, Drummond clarified. "The cats. The felines tie everything together, including the deaths at the different yoga clubs."

Hermon printed out one more label with the word *Cats* on

it and looked back at his partner. "Wood witch. You know I hate to get into that magic stuff. If I can't handle or touch it or put it in numbers on my computer, I just don't accept it."

Giving his partner one of his half-smiles, Drummond put down the labels on the table. When he was done, he stepped back and looked at his work with a satisfied expression.

"Now, Hermon, this is our crime and what we need to solve."

Hermon slid out of his chair and stood beside him. He looked at the stacks and labels. "I don't understand. What are you trying to tell me?"

"This is all tied together by one man." Drummond put a hand on the empty space without any folders. "They all look like separate crimes, bombing by a mad customer, a reporter sneaking out on a big story, a vet who's missing, and a bunch of feral cats that the city is full of on every street. What ties them all together? One man by the name of Elroy Wilmor. A man who's so smart that the crimes don't even lead back to him."

Hermon shook his head. "Okay, big guy, you've me lost. Who the hell is Wilmor?"

"We got a report from Detectives Ronson and Forrest." Now Drummond was searching through folders under the table. Hermon chuckled behind him.

"Here it is. They investigated the strange death of Pierce Connors in a company that, if you check what they own and then down the line, you find a new company of Yoga Health Centers just opening up. Now, the place where all the six deaths happened in yoga clubs was the opposition to the new center that's opening up. In this report, Elroy Wilmor was promoted to take the place of the dead, Mr. Connors. There was a cat at the Connors' death scene." Drummond laid the folder he'd found down on the table.

"Cats. That doesn't make sense." Hermon took the file and

95

returned to his computers. He typed in a few numbers and had more information on the crime from the detectives involved. "Partner, what's the meaning of the cats?"

"Well, my good friend, it has to do with that thing you don't like, witchcraft. I also think the vet got mixed up in this by error. She just took in the cats and did some special work on the ones involved with the crime areas. It got her targeted, and now she's missing."

His long fingers working fast, Hermon had information on Sarah Aggar up on one of the other screens. "So, Sarah's innocent and may have been kidnapped by whoever's behind all of this mess? Damn."

"You're right. But she's important to me, so I want to make her the top of my list." His voice was now low and husky.

"Okay, I'll build a new schematic. Something that I'll understand and can make sure our captain understands why we're chasing cats and some strange wood. Tell me where we start?"

"We go and tail a very important man." With those words, Drummond nodded that they should leave. It didn't take them long in the dark red car to find the apartment building that housed Elroy Wilmor. Having done some unusual checking, they'd found that he was home and owned an expensive black car. Checking with his laptop, Hermon said that the strange man was still up in his apartment, so they waited on the street. Drummond felt that they needed to find where he had any special properties. If he had the reporter and Sarah held in some safe place, it wouldn't be in his name.

He knew that didn't mean Hermon was willing to give up trying to trace anything that might lead them to where the two people might be detained. Hunting puzzles on the computer and through records was what he lived for. They had nothing to tie this executive into any of the crimes except for one meeting that Drummond had with Wilmor. That meant they needed some proof and someone else that the business-man had hired. The hired hand would be the weak link.

What this meant was that the two detectives were going to miss a lot of sleep and do some fancy work. They needed to trace this man's every move. Fortunately, in this day and age, there weren't many secrets. With Hermon's fancy computer, there were street cameras, on homes, and on businesses. There were GPS units on cars, phones, and computers.

CHAPTER SEVENTEEN

Elroy smiled as he went to the office first thing in the morning. He ordered breakfast from his favorite deli to be delivered to his desk, which was normal. He knew the strange big detective and his partner were watching. They weren't as smart as they thought. They were going to be bored today.

Again, like other criminals in the past, Drummond knew Wilmor was misjudging them. The two detectives made a point of getting exactly four hours of sleep after they made sure that the man they were watching had gone to work. Then they woke refreshed and started doing what each of them did, with their own special talents.

Hermon let him know that he'd hacked into places that would get them into federal prisons. That included Hermon tracing where the Wilmor's luxury car had been visiting over the last two weeks.

With the places that had been repeated, Drummond went in and installed small cameras. That meant that they now had cameras inside restaurants, parking lots, at two different office buildings, and a bank. For such a tall, handsome man, Drummond had a way to get into busy places and set up cameras without drawing attention to himself. It was a magical charm thing. After that, Hermon met him back in the *Charger*.

It took them the full afternoon while Wilmor was up in his office. Drummond noted that Wilmor worked late, and he'd ordered a light supper from a local restaurant. It had been a busy time for both because they'd done their jobs.

Like Wilmor, they ate a hearty meal, picking it up from a fancy deli in the area of Wilmor's office building. Eating in the car was something that was normal for them. Hermon was careful to see that everything was gathered up and put into one trash bag. He was a fussy person, but Drummond loved his partner.

It was full dark, after nine at night, before the suspect wrapped up his office work and came down the elevator, directly to the inside parking area.

Letting the luxury car come out of the big exit area onto the street, Drummond let a couple of cars get between them before he pulled out. They followed Wilmor for a few blocks and lost him as he pulled down a narrow street to turn into traffic. Drummond stayed on their road, full of people going shopping or to fine restaurants. It was one of those types of areas.

With the fancy metal-encased laptop on his knees, Hermon was watching a funny red dot travel on a strange map on the screen.

"He's traveling south on Fielding Avenue," Hermon said, while Drummond was busy moving through the traffic. "This is a route that he takes frequently."

"How often?" Drummond wondered.

"At least five times in the last two weeks. I can't tell you more without losing him." Hermon dropped the double screen and concentrated on just the map with the moving dot. "He's going over a couple of blocks now."

Drummond took the next left and moved through two blocks before turning south, still not close to Wilmor's car.

"Oh, I think I know where he's going. That parking lot that doesn't make any sense because it's not near any of the office buildings where he meets people." Hermon still let the dot move on the screen. "Right as predicted, Wilmor's dot disappeared into a garage." Now Hermon began working on a different site, and Drummond stepped on the gas. By the time the mighty police car in disguise was parked near the indoor multi-level parking garage, Hermon had a view on the screen.

It was from a camera that Drummond had deposited inside the lot. The view was not good, as there were very few lights inside the low ceiling of the section that they were watching. Hermon might have wondered how his partner had decided where to put the single camera. When Drummond entered this garage, he'd used his wizard strength and was surprised to feel an aura of magic. It was dark magic, evil, and it drew him. It wasn't the type that said a presence was there, just that something passed through and left an odor. That was the place to plant a camera.

In the dim light, they were watching Wilmor transfer those wrapped packages of water from the trunk of his car into the back of an open SUV. The man closed the trunk and hit his handheld lock, and the lights did a quick flash, letting the owner know the car was locked. The perp then went and got into the big *Cadillac* SUV and backed out to take an exit on the opposite side.

"Damn, I need to pick him up on street cameras until we get a license plate number off that big boat." Hermon was working the keyboard, and he had four screens showing cars moving.

Drummond was also in action, shadowing the car from just a block on one side as he tried to check down between streets, hoping to keep the car in sight on the other avenue.

"Gotcha'." Hermon had a photo shot up in one of the four screens. He had the back plate of the car, and as he enlarged it, the number was easy to read, even from his side of the car. He cleared the screen and was into the state's records. He went fast through record after record and found what he was looking for—a record on the plate number.

"It's a car owned by the company that Elroy Wilmor works

for, Bildof Investments. Now give me a couple of seconds, and I'll have the GPS up on that car." Hermon always only needed seconds.

It was back to the illegal hacking of satellites that followed and watching anything that responded to the Global Positioning System or GPS. The problem was with the millions of such items out on the earth, Hermon had to find a particular one that had its own digital code. Thankfully, Hermon was good. He soon had a map up and a silly little red dot crawling over the screen. "Okay, buddy, we're heading south. You can back off, and if you want, you can move over to Hamilton Street. That's the one he's on, but we can stay far enough behind so that he'll never know that we're following."

It was a long drive through the poor part of the city. The south side had fallen on bad times with empty buildings and crime out in the streets. Eventually, the river turned to wrap around and divide the city. The section was now small industry and large storage. The crime had tried to move into this dark region, but truckers and union workers had made small-time punks find it hard to mug or threaten these organized workers. At night, the locality wasn't busy. The large semis were slowly gathering at well-lit gas stations that had restaurants and even shower spaces attached. These ample precincts were like some alien zones of clean and safe places, where even a cop car or two was parked up near the brightly-colored central building.

Down among the tall metal buildings of storage and small businesses, there were intermittent tall lights. These still left deep shadows within the wide alleys between the structures. There were some attached illuminations to the front of the property over or by certain doors. These lights attached above the doors had been put up by the individual renters. Some had died since the companies within had also ceased to be in business. There was strange litter and debris down among these wide driveways. Not the small debris found on the south side poor streets. What was left to rot here in this district were containers, cartons, old metal pieces of machines, and even some rusting vehicles.

All of the leftover elements had been pushed up against cement barriers or the tin of the closest structure. The wide separations were clean for the big eighteen-wheelers to move down, turn, and back up to unload. There was a necessity for the deliveries and the trucks to move and pass each other.

There was no special entrance or exit to this part of the south end of the city. Some of the long, wide divisions between buildings just started or emptied onto the main streets that ran through the district. There were even places where a driver could turn off a street between the buildings that seemed to divide the long lines. All of the groups of construction weren't attached, so some groups were separated. There were some breaks in the type of construction—the height, whether there were windows, or just large overhead doors, or many smaller doors. It was a strange growth of what people needed and what an investor was willing to establish.

One thing was positive about the area. Even with some of the structures empty, it was still a thriving zone that stored or produced products. It was mostly full of things that moved through and didn't stay long in this area. It also didn't give much employment to the people in the south part of the city.

The businesses that were running full-time throughout the day were looking for trained employees with clean records. Most were hiring from the union halls to avoid problems. Let the unions vet the workers or keep the cheap street youths out of the mix.

CHAPTER EIGHTEEN

Drummond voiced his questions, wondering what the hell a high-paid company executive was doing, driving an expensive SUV down into this dark industrial locale. The red dot pulled in at the second truck stop, and Drummond drove past to watch Wilmor go into the restaurant. It was busy with the side lot full of the big rigs parked overnight.

"How about a greasy hamburger?" Drummond took the *Charger* onto another highway and into another well-lit stop with flashing signs that provided a home away from home for the long hauls. Here was where drivers could sit and exchange tales or tell what highways to avoid for many reasons. There were a couple of other reasons to be here, even with the highway patrol cars parked in front of the restaurant.

There were clean ladies of the night, or day, or whenever they were needed. Their pimps brought them over in vans that wouldn't attract attention. The ladies were higher on the chain than the ones in the city that stood on street corners.

The pimps stayed in the van, eating a meal one of the girls brought out to them. They played games on cellphones or pads but kept an eye on the ladies. They protected their commodities. The only time the girls would go inside was to pick up food or coffee, always one at a time.

Pulling the dark red car into a spot right in front of the windows of the eating sector, the detectives got out of the car. The lights reflected off the polish on the double clear coat that Drummond always kept on the paint job.

Two truckers walking by stopped and admired the car as

the partners got out.

"Nice. Original?" one younger man with a short beard asked as he stepped closer to admire the deep red hood.

Shaking his head, Drummond frowned. "Unfortunately, no. It's a recovery. But the engine and undercarriage are original."

"No shit! Is it a *Hellcat*?" Now both men were interested.

Not waiting, as he walked ahead with his computer, Hermon was more interested in getting online than the car. "Different strokes for different folks."

Drummond and the two drivers talked for a couple more minutes and parted. They were happy to talk about oil and tires. Drummond understood that his partner was more into a network than a throttle. Looking around inside the busy eating establishment, Drummond found Hermon was starting to sit down at a booth in front of one of the windows.

"I guess this is the route he'll take if he is heading south or going into the industrial park," Hermon said as he set up his laptop.

A waitress came over to their booth immediately — knowing that most of the people who came in here would need to order fast.

"Menu or standard?" Her question meant that would they need a menu to order from, or would they take the standard item that everyone ate when coming into this place. Several paper posters advertised the largest burgers in the city. Drummond ordered two of the standard plus a large salad while his partner worked. He also let the woman fill their cups with rich black coffee. Every driver would leave here and have his thermos filled with this brew.

It was two hours later, and a couple of pieces of apple pie with vanilla ice cream on the side, and they still waited. The red dot hadn't moved.

"Either he got into another vehicle, or this is a meet and

greet out in the middle of nowhere." Drummond thumped his knuckles on the table.

"So, what do we do now?" Hermon was hunting for street cameras. They were sparse out here, but there were cameras at each of the truck stops. Safety was important to the truckers and the owners. "The cameras inside only cover the different cash register areas and the two doors. On the outside, the entire area is covered, and his car is still in the same place."

Drummond was pulling some cash out of his pocket. "Maybe we need to go back and check out his car and the other restaurant to see if he's still there."

"Wait, I see him at the cash register. Look." Hermon twisted the laptop, and Drummond was looking at a blurry picture of the top of the head of a man paying a clerk his bill with a credit card.

They took two carry-out cups of coffee and went to their car to follow the red dot. As expected, the red dot went into the large maze of the industrial park. Weaving back and forth between the broken-up driveways or wide areas between the buildings, Drummond let Wilmor get ahead and come to a stop. He depended on Hermon's special computer to indicate where the big SUV was parked. Drummond pulled the *Charger* up to what he assumed was the opposite side of the same building.

This didn't have a back entrance to the place that Wilmor was using. It contained an active business with a sign over the small door that said something about Imports. There were lights on the wall of the building here over the small door and up over the tall roll-up door.

Sitting and thinking, Drummond leaned back in the seat and let out a huff. "I need to see what's happening."

"Well, our perp's unloading items from the SUV and taking them into the unit where he's parked."

Looking over at his partner, Drummond looked at the

screen that Hermon turned in his direction. Evidently, he'd found a camera on the outside of a nearby building. It gave them a view of the parked SUV and a man taking some items from the back seat. He left the back door open as he went into the building with his load.

Hermon frowned. "Why would a man be taking food and water into a unit marked *Storage*?"

"Yep, I think we need to do some detective work."

Drummond started up the engine and jerked the car into reverse. Taking the car in reverse down and around a corner, and then the next, pulling up behind a large trash container on wheels. He had the rear bumper up against the large receptacle that was taller than the car.

"Hermon, tell me when he finishes and closes up everything. Oh, and hang on tight to your computer." He purposely put a warning in his voice.

Looking around, Hermon asked, "Uh, partner, is this safe?"

"Hey, buddy, we only live once. Tell me when he's done." Drummond was gripping the leather steering wheel lightly.

Hermon's face was lit up by the reflection of the screen.

"I'm not sure I want to tell you this. But he's inside, and the car's locked up. It seems he got everything unloaded and . . ." Hermon stopped talking as the car began moving, still in reverse, pushing the large trash bin.

Drummond was looking out through both side mirrors as he made a big swing out to sling the car and its bumper toy around. He floored the peddle, and the heavy underframe, along with the big engine, had the car and its unusual load moving too fast for the tight area.

With a shudder that hit both passengers, they were through the wide overhead door and deep within the building. Drummond slammed on the brakes, stopping the car and letting the container continue. It came to a loud stop when it slammed into something solid that didn't move.

"Stay hidden until I take care of the dangerous guy," Drummond yelled out at his partner as he was getting out of the car and moving around the front hood. He felt the sting of evil and knew the man was startled — but ready to fight.

It was dark inside the building except for the lights from the car that were reflected from the front walls. But Drummond didn't need light to find a wood witch. The question was — would the man stay and fight, or would he disappear? This was a special lair for Wilmor, and important things were hidden within this building that might tie him to crimes. The courts would be happy to have concrete evidence on a man as high up in society as Elroy Wilmor.

"Too late." That was the cry that Drummond heard from a voice that was outside of the building. He ran as hard as he could and was out through the busted door to see nothing. There were no shadows moving, but the big SUV was still waiting quietly. Wilmor was gone. That was the way of a wood witch. *Damn.*

It wasn't long before the wide alley was full of flashing lights as everyone responded to the call from Detective Hermon Smith. Among the big trucks was an EMT unit waiting for whoever was in the four big safes sitting side by side in the warehouse.

Working around the techs that were getting the first door open was the CSI group checking the outside for traces and fingerprints. Other detectives were down at the office with not only the night clerk but a sleepy manager. They were going through the papers on the rental agreement on the large unit D27E. Another CSI clique was working on the SUV. Hermon was making copies of the camera shots of the truck stop with Wilmor and the SUV in them.

Everyone was working, but most were shaking their heads in a negative manner. The CSI groups were coming up with no fingerprints or trace evidence.

A holler came from one of the techs at the first big door. Drummond had been breathing down their collars as they worked, so he helped pull up the heavy bar. Now they tugged the door open, and a man staggered out, covering his eyes from the bright lights.

"Fuck, you better be the police," the man mumbled as he leaned forward.

Catching him, Drummond held him. "Okay, we're the police."

"Yes, hey, there's someone in the next metal box. Get them out right away." The man in Drummond's arms weakly pointed at the other vault. Looking at who he was holding, the detective realized it was the reporter. One of the street cops yelled over his shoulder for emergency help for the reporter. Soon, an EMT squad forced Milligan down on a rolling cot and hooked up a cuff on his arm.

The techs and Drummond were already working on the next door, hoping they would get in faster. The idea was that they'd learned from the last one. It was near dawn when the same tech nudged his buddy. "We got it opened."

Again, Drummond helped pull the lever and stood back as the door swung open. Unlike Milligan, Sarah was hesitant as she slowly stepped forward, also shielding her eyes.

"It's me, baby," Drummond said in a low voice as he moved up and slowly wrapped his arms around the tall woman.

"Oh, thank God. I knew you would find us." She allowed herself to sink into his arms as she spoke.

Reaching down, he put an arm under her knees and lifted her bridal style.

Her voice was harsh, probably from yelling, "There's another one locked up."

"Shhh, baby. We found him first." By this time, he had her

at the back of the big red and white emergency wagon. A woman jumped out and immediately helped set Sarah on the back floor with her legs outside. A cuff was attached to her arm as a bottle of water was handed to her. Drummond caught the water to uncap it, now giving it to Sarah. There was no conversation while the trained Paramedic did her work on the vet.

"I'll be right back." Drummond nodded and turned around to check on Hermon. It was obvious the skinny detective was in an argument with a couple of detectives or investigators.

"I'm telling you this shot is of Elroy Wilmor at the cash register at the truck stop. He's an executive at Bildof Investments, and that SUV is leased by them." Hermon was showing the picture from inside the truck stop.

The investigator walked away as he talked over his shoulder. "It'll never stand up in court. It's just looking down on the head of a guy. The guy's lawyer will laugh us out of court. We need some better pictures than that."

Their captain had shown up about an hour ago, and someone had handed him a phone. He looked around with a frown and handed the phone back. His next words that Drummond heard were just foul. Something was wrong. Staying by his partner, Drummond watched the captain walk across and around all the people in the big warehouse. He approached the two of them and the rest of the group of investigators.

"Bildof Investments has just called in a report of a car they lease that's been stolen. It's missing from its parking spot in their reserved lot below their building." Their captain looked like he was eating some of Drummond's matches while they were still on fire. The angry man turned and walked back out to where the CSI unit was going over the big SUV. Drummond followed to hear what was going on or what had been found.

The report was negative. No fingerprints, no traces, no fibers, and the car was spotless. They would have it towed in and taken apart to see if there were any missed items inside the carriage or underneath.

Turning, Drummond hurried back inside to the gal who was heading up the CSI unit inside. When he approached, she just shook her head.

"This is the cleanest warehouse I've ever been in. Someone went over this place with a power hose. See here." She took him over in her floppy blue safe-cover shoes to a wall. "See the marks from the power sprayer and the damage it did to the metal? The speed and pressure were almost too much. There are places where it pushed the wall away from the frame."

She was showing him what she was referring to with walls too clean. There was no dust, no debris, and no spider webs, no matter how high up Drummond looked into the ceiling of the warehouse.

Pointing at the four vaults, he asked, "And those?"

"Immaculate. Like the day they were built. Except for the remains of the two people inside the first two. The third and fourth are clean and spotless. This guy scares me, detective."

"Well, lady, when I catch up with him, I'm going to scare him. Mark my words because he went after someone close to me. Big mistake."

CHAPTER NINETEEN

Knowing when to take time and make the right decisions, Drummond and Hermon had gone home to sleep for about ten hours. This would let them dive into their puzzle and solve it with clarity. It was the way they worked together. Now they were back in their office doing the tedious police work. They were tracing everything connected to the warehouse on one computer and everything connected to Elroy Wilmore on another. They'd already done long interviews on both Milligan and Aggar. Both had refused to stay in the hospital and declined police protection.

Black and whites had been assigned to both parties. The reporter had lost his almost immediately, going into the newspaper office and disappearing. No surprise there, as the reporter was pissed and wanted to investigate his own story.

As for the vet, she went home and waited for all the hardware to be changed in her house. She had two pit bulls from one of the hospitals brought over to live with her. She closed all the drapes and disappeared in her own way, only talking to her people at the animal hospital and to Drummond.

The two captives had very little to tell. Sarah had been taken from her apartment, and the reporter was taken from his car. A gas was introduced that knocked them out. It was the same gas in both cases. Forensics identified the gas but found no trace of the abductor.

"Are you going down to talk to forensics?" Hermon wasn't typing, which was unusual.

"No need. They'll just tell me they haven't found any traces anywhere. I'm tired of hearing that repeated." Drummond slumped down in the chair and looked at the separate piles on the back table. "Why aren't you working on your keyboard?"

"I have a puzzle I can't solve." Hermon pointed at one end screen. In the middle was an old-fashioned crossword with the squares and the blacked-out sections. Right in the center was the word Elroy across, and running down was Wilmor using the *o* for each word.

"Talk to me, partner." Drummond turned and faced the one person he trusted.

"I know that we saw him get in his car and go to the location of the SUV. Even though the view from that camera is so dark, it's hard to get a good identification for the courts, I know it's Wilmor." Now he pointed to another screen and punched up a view of the man frozen with the water in his arms behind the vehicles.

"We both know this was Wilmor at the truck stop." Hermon split the same screen and had up the photo of the top of the head of the man paying at the cash register next to the dark garage photo. "This is Wilmor, unloading at the warehouse." Now, there was a third still photo on the same screen.

"I've run these through every photo progression process out there, including what NASA uses. I can't clear any of them up enough to prove a positive ID." Now Hermon flopped his long fingers down on the table.

"Okay, buddy, chase the money." Drummond tapped the crossword screen. "How does a ghost rent a warehouse, buy very expensive vaults, and hey, how does he hire a company to move those heavy fuckin' loads?"

"Cash and credit cards in unknown names." Now Hermon let his fingers fly on his keyboards. On the larger screen in front of him, he brought up some searches and had some strange information.

"Do you know how many places there are where a person can safely put cash, getting it out of reach of the IRS, and search for names or any IDs? There are so many more that Switzerland is being put out of business." Hermon mumbled as fast as he typed.

Now the thin man continued, "Everyone knows about the Cayman Islands, but now there's Brazil, and a lot of people look at Venezuela and Peru. There's Monaco. There are also some beautiful places to visit, like Antigua and Barbuda and Bahrain. Try finding out if there's money being hidden in the banks in those small places. There's also Cyprus and Malta. I could go on and on. All it takes is a lot of money, several million or more." Hermon quit typing and threw his hands up in exasperation.

"Worse of all, there are rumors that the Vatican Bank accepts outside deposits with a great deal of secrecy. Who knows since the code of confidentiality would keep anyone from finding the details." Now Herman had those long fingers over his eyes.

Now Drummond was sitting upright, but he was frowning. "So, Wilmor can have lots of cash hidden anywhere in the world and do with that cash just about anything he wants to, including buying four expensive vaults."

"Yep. Like I said, I think I've met a puzzle I can't solve." At last, Hermon looked through his fingers at the busy screens.

"Well, little buddy, I have a way to solve it, but you won't like it and can't come with me." With that, Drummond got up and grabbed his leather jacket. They'd spent a week on hopeless searches, interviews, and talking to other detectives. Drummond decided it was time for a different type of action.

The first thing he had to do was go into an unusual small shop in a different part of town to make a special purchase.

CHAPTER TWENTY

If someone asked Drummond to describe the shop, it would be interesting. It was a little curio store tucked in among all the same cloister of storefronts in this old part of town. These three and four-story buildings, though built almost a hundred years ago, were solid, erected when people took pride in their work, and things were meant to last. There were carvings and signature designs on each of the tall, narrow structures as they tucked in against each other, making a solid edifice for the entire block.

Age, along with the weather, had turned everything dark, but the patina was almost necessary to make people understand the importance of the dark beauty that comes after years of good use. This street still had the old black streetlights, with pale yellow gleaming that didn't insult the feeling of wise maturity on this roadway.

The shop was a permanent part of the lane, as was the bookstore, the shoe cobbler, and the coffee shop that sold real Columbian hand-ground with cream delivered at the back door from the country. The windows of the shop were low with not too many displays on the beautiful old scarves, tossed about to create a picture of soft dark colors. There were some fat candles, a couple of gold plates, a few beads, and some books piled at the back. The shop was darker within, so he couldn't see more than the display as he stopped to read the posted signs. The signs announced speakers at the local library or a séance at a local Reader's room. Yes, there was a Reader's room in the block.

The dark inset door had a dusky glass with brass accouterments. The brass was tarnished to a nice used patina that matched the blackened solid wood that held the glass. In the middle of the glass was the only identification of the shop, the local address of nine six three in old-fashioned Anglican type style. When he did find a reason to enter the shop that bore only the number but no name, a pleasant, soft tinkle of a bell rang out. Then he got all the smells that changed as he moved slowly within the aisles.

It was strange as people told different stories of their reactions to the street and the door of the shop. Some said they didn't remember a shop there at all. Many said display windows always drew them to read whatever new sign had been posted or look to see if anything new had been added to the displays. Yet, a few said they couldn't walk past the little shop without going in past that beautiful old door.

Drummond stood in front of the door with the faded gold numbers, nine six three. This time he was alone without his partner, and he missed Hermon already. They both did what they excelled at, even if others didn't understand them. What counted was that they got results.

The glass was dead, but the large cat was sitting, looking at him through it was alive. Drummond realized the cat could've been there all along since it was midnight black. Until it moved, no one would see it in the dim light of the glass corner of the window. The night was alive.

What Drummond really saw were the two startling light green slanted eyes staring at him without a blink. Green eyes that sucked in the light to reflect back at whoever she looked at as she stared in the dark. Clever. He stood here now, glancing back at his large shadow in a reflection, knowing that he'd be the one to go into the shop ruled by a black cat. Black cats weren't bad luck. He took a deep breath of the thick wet air and entered the shop.

Above his head were the soft tinkles floating, similar to snowdrops in the air from the bells that the door hit as it moved. The sound was pleasant to the ear, but Drummond looked up to admire the small set of gold that settled down as soon as the door swung shut behind him with a solid click. This was what Drummond did. He looked at the details.

Here, though, in this shop, there were too many details. They pulled at him. He took a couple of steps into the dimly lit aisle to see cabinets and shelves and glass cupboards everywhere, details that pulled at his soul. They were all units, highboys, China cabinets, and rows over rows of holding spaces. Holding spaces were full of details.

The problem for Drummond was that everything was full—full of candles of every size, shape, and color. There were even candles burning here and there. Beyond the candles, there were jars full of items that Drummond had no idea what they contained. There were small ones, large ones, clear ones, and crude clay-fired urns sitting next to beautiful oriental vases. For him and his details, many of the jars stood in front of others, the dim shadows of rows of what he needed to know.

Drummond's eyes strayed across the beautiful articles that he recognized. These were different types of feathers in bunches. Then there were beads and chains all in reflective glows either hanging or flowing from small bowls.

At last, as he moved slowly back into the shop, he smelled and saw the roots and wood items. If someone had the time to go through all of the hundreds on display, would some be illegal? In the pale flickering of the candles, with the sweet smell of some of the dried berries and leaves, there was a draw to pick up one here, to look closely at one there. Drummond's twitchy fingers moved, but he resisted.

Hearing a noise, he jerked at the thought of someone catching him as he'd almost picked up a piece of wood. He turned fast in the dim, tight aisle with everything closing in around him. The cat was there. He tried to move as he and the cat danced around each other. The cat won the dance contest when she twisted around in the tight quarters, missing Drummond's shoes and bouncing once off his left leg. Then she leaped through the beaded curtain at the end of the aisle. The same movement allowed him to move gracefully.

Finally, Drummond's brain kicked in as his eyes followed the place where the cat had disappeared. A woman dressed as a gypsy came out to smile.

"Master, how may I serve you?" She did a small bow as she spoke, recognizing the wizard as a special person in the magic world.

"I need something extremely special. I have the price in gold." Drummond smiled. Wilmor wasn't the only one to have hidden assets. He opened his hand, which held a large gold coin.

"Please come this way, master." The woman led him back through the narrow aisles, past all the samples and beautiful displays. Going into the back room, an attractive woman in her early fifties greeted him.

"Welcome, master. Please have a seat." This area held a table covered in a damask cloth and was only lit with many candles. Drummond knew that at one time, the shop was owned by a beautiful white witch. He'd an affair with her, but she was long gone.

"Mistress, I need a bit of root from an ancient American chestnut tree."

"Ah, a very rare tree. The younger sprouts are dying from blights. The ancient ones are hidden among large old groves of other trees high in elevations about seventeen or eighteen hundred feet."

Lying the gold coin on the table with his ring finger on it, showing both the large piece of metal and his special ring. The horns on the ring could be either a warning or a protection symbol.

The woman nodded. "It will be a small piece of root."

"It's all I need." Drummond pushed the coin forward and left it in the middle of the table.

With this, the woman got up and went behind her to a tall cabinet full of small drawers without handles. She just stood there for a short time, and one of the drawers slid open. Reaching up, she drew out a red cloth that wrapped something.

Returning to the table, she sat down and looked directly at Drummond. Slowly, the woman exchanged the gold coin with the small red cloth package and bowed her head, mumbling a small enchantment.

Looking up at him, she smiled. "Go in peace, wizard."

"May peace be with you, mistress." Drummond gathered the red cloth with a small odd piece of root wrapped inside. Now he was ready to go out and meet a ghost. He was sorry that he had to leave his awkward friend behind, but it wasn't safe for the clumsy thin geek.

Besides, the geek continued to state that he didn't believe in magic and wouldn't like to see what was going to happen next. The hunt was on, and Drummond knew where to look. This monster wouldn't be in his office or even that expensive apartment. He'd be gathering his crew and purchasing some other big items that Wilmor thought would help him take over the city, the state, and then who knew what else he had in his designs.

He needed to drive Wilmor out, so he had his partner do one thing. He made one quick call to Hermon. "Buddy, I have the proof. Tell the captain and put out an arrest warrant on Wilmor."

"Great. What did you find?" He could hear Hermon typing even as he talked in his excitement.

"I'll bring it all in later. Just take my word for it and get that warrant out before the guy slips out of the city." Drummond regretted lying to his partner, but he believed when it was all over, he'd have proof of Wilmor's funds and crime in the city. They'd find his hidden apartment, and the place Drummond knew he had out in the woods.

Pulling out of a gas station just at the edge of the down-town area, Drummond took his time driving with the traffic. He now had a full tank of gas and an extra-large coffee in the holder in the center section. He was watching the parking lot where Wilmor's luxury car was still sheltered on the bottom floor. Finally, that big car pulled out onto the wide avenue, but Drummond could tell from the outline of the person driving that it wasn't Wilmor.

Making a decision, Drummond followed the decoy. But at the first side street, he turned off and pulled into the curb to watch in his rearview mirror. Now he saw the black and white moving up to follow the same car. He decided it wouldn't take long for the cop car to turn on the lights.

Waiting for a break in the traffic, he made a U-turn and was back out on the avenue among the traffic. Listening to his gut feeling, he turned back just in time to see another *Cadillac* SUV pulling out from the garage and going in the other direction. He slipped the *Charger* in behind several other cars and watched the high back of the expensive car. He didn't doubt that Wilmor would only drive another high-priced vehicle.

This was going to be a long night, as Drummond sipped his coffee and made sure there were plenty of cars in front of him to hide his low vehicle. They drove through the early night traffic for over half an hour. Thinking he'd given the cops long enough to find out who was in the first car, he made a call.

"This is Detective shield nine-four-two out of district twelve. Sighted wanted person on notice issued Twenty-One

119

B on Fletcher Ave. going north in *Cadillac* SUV. Tag Two-VB-four-eight-four."

"Confirm." The voice came back on the radio, and it was only about three minutes that Drummond heard the sirens coming up behind him. Like the cars around him, he pulled over to the curb. But he actually got out of the car and started down the sidewalk.

Wilmor was smart. He must have had a radio in the SUV to pick up the cop calls. He left the big bulk in the street, blocking several other vehicles, including a delivery truck, and was out. With a gun that Drummond could barely see, he hijacked the car in front and was gone before the two patrol cars with blue lights flashing were on the scene.

Drummond was back in his car and had all the hidden lights up and flashing. He pulled around all the stopped vehicles and drove down the wrong way until he was past the blockage. Now he turned off his blazing lights and stayed back behind the sedan that was now a block ahead.

CHAPTER TWENTY-ONE

Almost losing Wilmor, Drummond found it hard to stay hidden and yet follow the evil man. Now, even though he hated to involve his partner, he called Hermon.

"Hey, where you at?" There was a smile in Hermon's voice.

"I need your help with cameras. If you have the police views up, you know that the cops are closing in on Wilmor." Drummond was watching traffic and trying to keep track of the sedan.

"Are you in the middle of that chase? Wait, I just caught a glimpse of the *Charger* on the wrong side of the road. Damn."

Drummond's voice was urgent. "Yes, Wilmor's in a grey sedan. He hi-jacked it. Can you get any eyes on it?"

Drummond heard the clacking as Hermon used his keyboard and skill to hack into street cameras, sitting at a desk in police headquarters miles away. "Got him. He ran a red light on Wilmington and Fifth."

"Okay, I'm behind him. Hermon, we don't want him caught. We need to herd him to his hide-out. Can you help me?"

There was a chuckle from Hermon. "Sounds like a game I used to play. Sure, I'll let you know where he's at, and I'll let the cops know where he was almost a few minutes ago."

"Yes, a deadly game." Now he knew he sounded deadly.

The car chase went on through traffic and traffic lights. It was fast and dangerous, with the wet streets and the other vehicles on the roads.

Then Hermon talked to him. "Problem. Cops have picked

up on the sedan speeding and him running the red lights. There's a couple of black and whites coming in ahead of him."

"Thanks." Drummond slowed down so he could watch to see what Wilmor would do next. Maybe this wouldn't be bad. It would send the panicky man closer to the western edge of the city. That was the direction Wilmor was heading in each turn. He was heading out of the city towards the west. Several blocks ahead of them, Drummond could see the police cars' distant flashing blue lights coming. The sedan smashed into another small car on purpose, pushing that car sideways into a van and causing a pile-up of more vehicles.

Wilmor was out of the sedan, running behind and stopping, pretending to help someone in a car at one side. Then he was around that car and walked with some others too where a big van was on its side. It was the one vehicle in front as the police cars pulled up. Everyone backed up, and Wilmor stayed in the small group as they moved out of the way of the cops.

Climbing on top of a hood with his badge out in his hand for all to see, Drummond tried to keep an eye on the elusive crime luminary. Wilmor was so smart that he blended in with the crowd and allowed the police to push them all back out of the way. He turned and moved over to a van that was stopped and sitting to one side with the commotion.

The vehicle only received a small tap on the side rear fender, and the driver was out with the crowd. Obviously, the man was waiting to report the small problem to the police just to have a report for his insurance.

With a sigh, Drummond was down and back to his car. He turned on the many hidden police lights and swung around the crash site. As soon as he was clear, he killed the blue and white flashing colors and stayed a couple of blocks behind the van. He contacted Hermon.

"Partner, he's in a van. It's light tan. Still on Wilmington.

Can you locate him?"

"Give me a sec." Hermon was hitting the keys so hard that the sound came through the speakers.

Drummond was driving carefully since there were fewer vehicles on the wide road now. Drummond was hoping that Wilmor didn't pick up on the fact that a deep red *Charger* was following him.

"Got it. Oh, he just turned south on Maxwell. That's a weird street. It'll move west in a big sweep in a few blocks."

"No problem." Drummond stepped on the gas and soon made the same turn. By that time, Wilmor was out of sight on the long street as it made the long turn.

"There's going to be a problem, big guy. If he keeps going at that speed and in this direction, he's going to get away from the traffic cameras. Also, that van is old and doesn't have GPS on it. I'm going to have difficulty helping you." There was worry in Hermon's voice.

"Understand. Just keep an eye on my car. If we get out to something you can identify, fill me in on the details." It was the only hope Drummond had since his car's GPS was loud and clear.

For the next couple of hours, the van drove through the shorter buildings to apartment units. Each of the units got smaller, and finally, there were houses, larger ones next to each other, and then the place where homes were only four or five on a block. This was the area where large trees hung over the roads, and the names on the signs were ancient ones, like Washington, Lincoln, and Martha. At last, in the dark, as the city marker ended, there were no longer lamps along the sidewalks.

The red taillights were often lost as Wilmor turned into long side roads that were forest-lined. It was about fifteen minutes when Drummond realized he'd lost the van. He stopped in the middle of the quiet road and thought about the last time he'd seen the van's red illumination. The road in front of him was open and clear, available to his eyesight by the reflection of the full moon overhead. He had no choice but to turn around and look for some turnoff or driveway.

"Hermon, tell me you can check with the satellite and see something that would hide Wilmor." Drummond needed his partner to make one more try. "I'll give you a hint. It'll be made entirely of wood."

There was a moment of silence and then a small chuckle. "You're in the middle of dumb fuck. That means all the buildings are made from wood. There are no big barns because that's a heavily forested sector. But there are small homesteads and cabins for hunters. There's a large old house that you passed on the road back behind you. It had been in one family for over a hundred years. I'm looking it up to see its history. I wonder why it's not been declared a Historical site since it is so old."

Turning the car around, Drummond listened to Hermon.

"Ah, I got it. This family is so old they fought in the Civil War, even though they were up here on the border's north side. I guess they believed in slave workers and, in modern times, would be members of the KKK. Except the last owners died off in nineteen-fifty-six, and the estate has been in contest in the courts looking for heirs ever since."

Hermon seemed confused. "Someone's paying the utility bills. Probably some lawyer who's found a way to get free money from a trust fund."

Finding the pull-off, Drummond saw that it wasn't used very often. The mailbox by the road was tilted and covered by weeds. He decided they didn't get much correspondence — even the flyers weren't left by the delivery service this far out in the country.

The center of the path that had tire marks was full of tall, dried plants that brushed against the bottom of his car. He kept all the wheels in the dry dust that led back under trees that cut out the moon and stars. The drive was a long, bumpy trip with Drummond hunched over the steering wheel, watching ahead. The headlights were only showing the weeds and lower branches. At last, the area ahead cleared, and now the moonlight let Drummond stop to see the tall old house that looked like something from a Stephen King movie.

It was two stories tall with gable windows poking through the roof and hadn't been painted in years. This wasn't one of the pretty ones with nice tall pillars. It just had a few steps leading up to a small, covered porch that led to the double front doors. Off to one side sat the van he'd been following.

It looked like, when new and painted in brown and navy, it was an ugly house, even in its best condition. It had been built to handle a large family and show the neighbors that this family had money at a time when it was rare.

Wondering how he was going to lure Wilmor out of the house, Drummond tapped his thumb on the steering wheel. He sat and pondered his problem. Finally, he took out a wooden match and put it in his mouth. It was time for action. Getting out of the car, he walked over to the van and stood for a moment, looking beyond it at the house. There were some low lights that shown in a couple of windows on the first floor and in one on the second floor. Drummond felt eyes on him from a dark window. It was time for action and magic.

Taking the wooden match out of his mouth, he tossed it in an arch into the open driver's side window, catching it on fire. This time not only did the match continue to burn, but as soon as it touched the seat, there was a large flash, and the entire inside of the van was in flames.

Drummond slowly stepped back to lean against the hood of the low red *Charger* that was still warm. It gave him comfort to feel the leftover heat from the *Hellcat* engine. Perhaps there was a little hell in the dark red car that he chose to drive. He needed all the help he could get from both sides of magic, black and white.

Chapter Twenty-Two

Drummond was glad that he'd left his partner behind, as Wilmor appeared with drama. The moon disappeared, and rain poured down from suddenly appearing dark clouds that fell with a hiss on the burning van. The next that came was lightning. A long streak lit up the dark trees and made the ground shake, but it didn't touch anything. Wilmor was standing on the bottom step, a long coat with the collar turned up to keep the rain off his neck.

By this time, Drummond had his leather coat uptight in the same manner, the big collar up around his head and chin. A little water didn't bother a master wizard, but he knew it was a toy for a wood witch. Calling up a protection ward, Drummond walked forward. There was a circle as if he had an umbrella over his head. When he got close to the front steps, Wilmor was gone.

Hearing the laughter behind him, Drummond turned to see the dark shape under the first trees' shadows, beyond the clear area. Now the war began. Going down on one knee, Drummond picked up a handful of wet dirt and leaves as he added a small word. He threw the dirt up into the air, and a bird materialized to fly immediately toward the dark figure. As the bird got close, limbs from the tree above reached down, and like strange hands, they grabbed at the bird. The bird disappeared, and the tree limbs turned to grey fog and blew away with the rain and wind. This was a battle of equals, unless something special happened.

Deciding he hadn't come out here to spend the night with

a criminal, Drummond reached into his pocket with one hand and pulled out a packet wrapped in a cloth. In the other, he sought and found another wooden match to stick into his mouth. Everything the two men created were just illusions. Most of the magic was fog, mist, and misconceptions to scare or frighten people, to make them do what was wanted. Sometimes, the reaction needed was to move, and again, it was just to upset the intended individual to get them distressed, raising their blood pressure. That character will then make a mistake.

For these two magical beings, the illusions they were throwing at each other were just a play, a toy to test each of them. Now, Drummond, the master wizard, decided it was time to play a real game. He uncovered the strange piece of root. It was clean and white in the moonlight since it had been pulled out of the ground and scraped down to the center of the wood. Pulling the match from his mouth and igniting it, Drummond brought a flame to the tip of the wood and placed it under the end of the root as he held it away from him with his thumb and forefinger.

"No." It was a scream from the dark figure at the edge of the forest. With those black outlined arms raised, Wilmor mumbled, and the rain was back—heavier.

Still, not a drop fell on the Drummond as he applied the heat to the root, watching it and ignoring the distant silhouette. Roots were hard, grew tight and tough, and wouldn't turn into a flame easily, but shrivel and slowly went up in smoke. Smoke came from the end of the white root that Drummond held out in front of him over the fire from the match. Even with the rain, the fire began on the trees around the figure. Drummond didn't like what he had to do, but it was the only way to defeat the wood witch. He had to destroy the forest that fed the evil man's illusions.

In Wilmor's misapprehensions, he was calling on black

magic, and that led only to one place. *Satan.* That evil was real and looked for any hole to reach in and seduce humans into sin. The sin that Wilmor would commit was to continue what Pierce Connors had started—killing any homeless male to leave a message to competition without thought.

To burn down a large quantity of old trees was a small price to pay in order to stop a man who was willing to take any steps to reach his desires. With his abilities, Drummond knew that Wilmor's desires were wealth, power, and eventually, a position as an elected official.

Lightning was now striking over and over, making Drummond's ears ring with the loud drumming noise. The dark shape of his enemy was shaking in anger as the storm increased. Still more trees and wood were on fire. This was the real magic told in the old tales. The special root was sending out its pain and the fire to the family nearby, putting all the woody plants up in a conflagration.

There were two things that were going to happen from this visible inferno. A weakened, suffering male was going to be on his knees, and firefighters with police would be at the location soon. All Drummond could do was mumble words from an old language and wait for an end to this scenario.

Wilmor screamed one more time and turned to run into the flaming forest. Now Drummond rose, dropping the match, moving close to the heat of the out-of-control fire on the trees and underbrush.

Within the brightness of red and orange colors, he could see Wilmor's clothes go up to rival the same fire as the trees. The man staggered deeper into the blaze as he yelled and screamed words that didn't make any sense. It seemed he was calling out to his father. At last, Drummond pulled back from the extreme temperature to shake his shoulders. There was no way to help the stumbling body that was fully engulfed in the fire as Wilmor fell flat within the drips of blazing items falling from above.

Going back, Drummond leaned against his car and waited. In the distance was the sound of sirens. The local firefighters were on their way.

Drummond watched as it turned to daylight—the smell of ash and dead things with a touch of wet ground left a cough in the back of everyone's throat. The type of firefighters who came to this forest fire were different than the ones in the city. These carried most of their equipment on their backs, and their trucks were big, tough, and could drive almost anywhere.

They found Wilmor's body and brought out the burnt remains in a black bag. The head superintendent was discussing with the local news that it was a miracle that the fire didn't spread, but it seemed to put itself out on new or wet growth.

Having talked to his partner through the car's hook-up, Drummond was waiting for a local cop and a warrant that would allow them to enter the house and seize pertinent paperwork or computers. A couple of state troopers were here at the sight, and they were friendly enough, but they didn't seem impressed with a big city cop on their territory. Hermon had already brought Drummond up to date with the fact that there was nothing to be found in Wilmor's apartment. The computer's hard drive was missing, and the only paperwork was bills and advertisements from the mail that had just been delivered.

Thinking of Wilmor, Drummond shook his head. The guy was so smart that he had money hidden all over the world, yet he committed suicide instead of being arrested. The two partners were worried that Wilmor had a gang that would still be in action. There might be someone out there, high enough or close enough to Wilmor, who might want all that money. Maybe they would do as much or more damage as

Wilmor because they didn't have his intelligence to keep everything hidden.

The warrant came, and Drummond entered the ancient house with several deputies and one man in a suit. He knew it was going to be interesting as soon as they got into the first room. Everything was covered with old drop cloths and dust and cobwebs. There were no footprints on the dusty floor except for the clean hallway that led up the stairs to the second floor. Every room they looked into had the same appearance, untouched for years.

It was the same uninhabited look on the second floor as the lack of prints in the dust before all the rooms with the doors open. The beds with no mattresses and all the standard furniture with the old covers hiding the shapes were all that could be seen. A couple of the deputies left their own footprints as they walked down the full length of the hall to check all the rooms. Nothing. Drummond just looked at the clean steps and went on up to the upper attic or third level.

Here, due to the roof's slope, the rooms just opened off to the large central square that went back to the rear of the roof. There was no guessing as to which way to go. Two rooms were clean and were being used on a regular basis. Glancing in one, it was a bedroom with a small bathroom off to one side, all open and lit by the light from the front's dormer window. It was the other room that Drummond was interested in, an office that also had one of the dormer windows. Here was all the high-tech equipment to make Hermon grin from ear to ear.

Several metal tables were set up to hold all the equipment along with keyboards, screens, flat boxes with tiny lights lit up, and some small standing strange antennas.

A guy in a suit walked around Drummond and moved close to the computers. "Well, it looks like we finally have some solid information." He reached out a hand and began to type as if he was trying to turn on the system.

"Hey, don't touch that." Drummond started to reach for the guy's arm, but the man kept his body in front of him to prevent him from interrupting what the man was trying to do with the computers. At that moment, the whole system sitting on the table blew up.

The blast threw the two of them across the small room and back out the door into the square hall. Fire and smoke filled the electronics as other officers began to run in their direction. With glass and flames bursting out through the front window, a couple of the firemen grabbed their equipment and were inside as fast as they could run. One deputy who was directly under the explosion on the second floor was buried under debris.

Others instantly began to pull him back and douse the fire from him with their jackets. One fireman stopped there and began to pump liquid to put out the last of the flames on the ceiling. The others continued up the stairs. Drummond was slowly pushing the man off of him as his hearing returned. He had some unusual glass and metal pieces in the one arm he'd put around the man.

There was no doubt that the man lying in front of him was dead. The guy had taken the full brunt of the explosion, receiving large amounts of pieces in his stomach. Blood was flowing freely around the man's guts that were exposed over his tight belt. There was no heartbeat with that gush of life liquid. In front of Drummond, the room was on fire. The walls and anything that was plastic had been affected by what was in the bomb that was hooked to the trap on the computer. By the time he could slide back to get away from becoming what had happened to Wilmor, he could hear someone on the stairs.

"Careful, everything's on fire, and the floor may be weak," he yelled out to warn whoever was coming up through the stairs behind him.

"We got this detective." One of the forest firemen came up the stairs in his complete outfit with packs on his back. He began pumping liquid in front of where the dead man was lying with his feet still in the damaged room.

Another fireman was still on the steps. "Hey, big guy, let's get you out of here." He moved and held out a hand to get Drummond down the stairs. "We need to get that arm looked after."

"No problem. Look after the fire first." Drummond was sorry for one thing—it bothered him to have his fine leather jacket so torn up in the arm.

CHAPTER TWENTY-THREE

Sleeping for eighteen hours was unusual for Drummond, but after having his arm stitched up in a couple of places, he needed the rest. The next thing he did was to go to a special tailor and get a new leather jacket. He was hard to fit with wide shoulders and narrow hips. The jacket had to be a long one, almost to his knees, and of the finest lamb. The cost was over eight thousand. He didn't regret the price. The feel of the soft leather that let him move with ease yet still turned the weather for the wet city that he prowled in each night was worth the bucks.

Now the partners were back where they started. Well, they did have some information, but it led nowhere. They knew Wilmor was the crime lord. They didn't know why, and they didn't know where all of his funds were hidden.

They sat together in their strange little side office and pondered the puzzles.

"What's the one thing that we have in all of these files?" Drummond was leaning back with his feet up on the back table. He nudged one of the stacks with his large boots.

"Cat hair," Hermon grumbled as he was brushing a sleeve. He then returned to his keyboard.

Suddenly, Drummond jerked upright. "Yes, you're brilliant."

"What?" Hermon also jumped at Drummond's strange reaction.

Drummond had a smile on his face. "I need to call Sarah. It's only nine-thirty. She'll still be awake."

Hermon turned and listened in confusion as he called the vet. After the usual friendly greetings, Drummond got down to the reason for the contact.

"Of all the cats you have in the isolation hospital from the crime scenes, did any of them come in with collars?"

Sarah's voice was clear through the cell phone. "Well, strangely, several of the cats had collars. There were no tags on any of the collars, and none of the cats had any implants for identification. Some of them were surprisingly clean."

Drummond looked over at Hermon and made a thumbs-up motion. "I don't suppose you kept any of the collars?"

"Well, of course, we did." Sarah gave a small laugh. "We kept all the debris from cleaning the cats in case the police needed the evidence."

"I love you." It was a shout from Drummond as he stood. "Where are the collars stored? I need to see them right away."

"Well, they're in the back of the main hospital in a locked closet. If it's important, I can meet you there now." Drummond was standing almost before she finished.

The decision was made that Drummond would go out and meet with the lady, and Hermon would stay with the large bank of hidden computers in the office. Drummond was sure that he'd have important information to relay back. It wouldn't take long to make the drive to the back of the building to meet Sarah.

Sarah had been reluctant to go out, even to work. She'd installed heavy locks and new doors on her home, along with an alarm and camera system. Now she came to meet her detective in a car driven by a bodyguard who was a retired cop. Her life had changed, and she didn't like it, but she'd survive. Drummond was waiting when they pulled around in the back of the big building.

"You can take a break. This will be about an hour," Sarah told her driver as she got out of the passenger seat. She refused to sit in the back of the car. It was bad enough to have someone drive her all of the time.

The tall detective was immediately by her side, one hand in the middle of her back in a protective mode. With a key in her hand, she opened the door, and they stepped inside, disarming the simple code on the pad on the wall. There were low lights in the hall, as she led Drummond down around a couple of turns. There was the smell of antiseptic and animals. At last, she pulled up her keys again and inserted one into the simple lock that was in the doorknob.

Opening the door, Sarah reached around and hit a switch to turn on a light to show a large storage area. It was full, but neat and systematic with shelves and boxes with labels on everything. There were even places with warnings and some with dates. Moving in, Sarah went back through a tight aisle to where metal shelving stood against the wall. On it were a couple of larger storage boxes. They were marked, and one had the label of the date and *Police Evidence*.

"Everything you might be looking for is in here." Moving out of his way, she allowed him to pull the box off the shelf. Sarah pulled out a small folded table at the front of the closet and set it up for Drummond. This allowed him a place to set the box down and open the lid. Inside were a bunch of items, all collected in sealed plastic envelopes.

She was smart and careful. Each see-through envelope was marked with a date, what cat the items had been retrieved from, and what the debris or items might have in a title. At last, on one side were the envelopes with the collars. Each one of the envelopes had the correct information in neat black letters.

Drummond twisted the collar without opening the first envelope until he could get it flat and checked to see if there was any writing on the old dirty leather.

"There were no names on any of the collars. I checked personally," Sarah said.

Drummond ignored her. He wasn't looking for names. On what would be the inside of the collar, he was looking for a couple of small numbers. The next collar didn't have anything on it. It was the two that he pulled out together that had numbers. He worked his way through the collars, and when he was done, he called his partner.

"Okay, Hermon, work your magic. I'm going to give you some numbers. I don't know if they're passwords, locations, or what. I've done my job, so now it's up to you and your computers. All we both know is that they're connected to Wilmor and his money."

He helped Sarah put everything back in order in the storage room and locked it up. Outside, he told her he was going to follow her home. Until they were sure they had all of Wilmor's mess cleaned up, he didn't want to take any chances with Sarah's safety.

Taking the time to walk her up to her front door, and both enjoying a long kiss, he finally left to go back to the office.

Once at the office, he just moved the pile of folders and watched Hermon playing with the figures.

Hermon tried latitude, hunting for storage areas, locations, or new forests. All of that was on one screen. He put the numbers into different lines on another screen and asked Google a simple question about whether that list meant anything.

It all seemed so frustrating and mind-blowing. There was no doubt that the nine numbers were important to Wilmor, but they could just be so many things to such a crazy mind like the wood witch. Drummond thought about magic and how the numbers would reflect in that genre. Six and thirty-six are important and must be carefully used in magic.

"What have you found for us, buddy?" Drummond looked over at all the different screens full of strange searches.

Clicking on the keys, Hermon shook his head. "What I haven't found seems more important. Nine numbers are crazy. First of all, there's no zero in the nine numbers, and none of them are duplicated except for the three. So, we really have ten numbers."

Turning a screen over for Drummond to look at closely, Hermon continued, "It can't be a latitude and longitude for anything. Those location finders are eight numbers long each or sixteen numbers altogether."

Now Hermon pointed at another screen. "If we turn to numerology, the number nine is important. The nine represents communicativeness, scale, universalism, and diversity, but if we add in the extra three, it throws out that scale."

There was a big screen right in front of Hermon that he referred to next. "So, here it gets worse. Wilmor's name has too many letters to make any number match. As for the nine plain numbers, they could be social security numbers. A scramble search comes up with eighteen possible matches. Of those, seven of the people are deceased. Five are retired, and it shows they're receiving their monthly payments in two other states. Two are teenagers, also out of state."

Speaking up to be part of what Hermon was doing, Drummond moved close to an active screen. "That leaves four, right?"

"Yep," Hermon agreed. "Let's do some surfing. Okay, here's the first one, a Mrs. Elanore P. Moorehead. She lives in Kentucky and takes care of the family while her husband, the local sheriff, works all his hours for the county."

Shaking his head, Drummond let out a snort. "Something tells me we can eliminate Mrs. Moorehead. Who do we have next?"

"A Hector Colon of Puerto Rico, living in Ohio now. A truck driver and on his second marriage that seems to be the happy one, with it over ten years. He's up to date on his child support payments to his previous wife and has nothing on his record. I think we can eliminate him also."

"Fuck, I need a drink." Drummond slid back, not satisfied with what he was seeing on the screens.

Sighing, Hermon put another name and ID up on a small screen. "Okay, the next guy's from the bordering state. He's Samual H. Morrison and is a state representative."

That information had Drummond's attention. "You know what, partner? I think we need to get in contact with Representative Morrison. Who's the last one?"

"Oh, it's Devon Michaels. A young black man in New York. And look here, he has quite a rap sheet for such a youth." The screen was full of small arrests for robbery and drug problems.

"No, the man of interest is Morrison."

Hermon continued to work. "So, do I quit looking at the numbers?"

Drummond looked at the screens and shook his head. "Even if Morrison's connected to Wilmor, the numbers mean something else. Keep running searches. You might find something like a password or a bank code. It might let us get into his Cayman Island safety deposit box."

With one partner on a keyboard and the other on a cell-phone—both detectives did their job.

CHAPTER TWENTY-FOUR

It was four in the afternoon before Representative Morrison called back. The call came in on Drummond's cellphone at his home inside a warehouse. He'd been asleep, but he was instantly awake and alert at the tone. Reaching over for the phone, he sat up on the side of his bed.

"This is Detective Drummond."

"Yes, this is Representative Morrison. I received a message that there was an important investigation that you needed to talk to me about. How can I help you?"

"Yes, Representative Morrison, sorry to bother you, but we're investigating the suicide of Mister Elroy Wilmor. Your name came up in going through his papers." Drummond was telling a lie since the representative's name hadn't shown up in anything connected with Wilmor.

"Did you say suicide? I'm so sorry. I didn't know the man very well. I think he did contribute to my re-election fund. I'm sorry. Besides that, I don't think I have anything to help you. If you need to follow up on this further, you'll have to go through my office and my legal advisor."

"Well, we can do that if it's necessary, sir." Drummond hesitated. "We'll call your office for an appointment. Thank you."

The man on the other end didn't even say goodbye. He just disconnected the call. Drummond smiled. He decided to go ahead and get up. This would give him time to take a long shower and clean some things up in this small home. He might even take some time to pay attention to Midnight, his cat. What he really ended up doing was adding an extra coat of wax to the dark red *Charger* sitting in the warehouse. Finally, it was time to go and pick up his partner and head for work.

Perhaps Drummond felt good about contacting Morrison, but his partner was almost hopping. Once Hermon was in the car, he had his computer open. "Look. Take the nine numbers minus one of the threes, put them together, and you get a phone number."

Drummond looked at the phone number on the screen. "How long did it take you to hunt through all the permutations to come up with that number, and what makes you think it might lead us somewhere?"

Chuckling, Hermon was like a kid. "I wrote a program and let it do the hunting. I don't want to tell you how many thousands of tries it went through to come up with about a hundred that made any sense. But I looked through the hundred and got one I thought you'd like. Still using only the numbers from the collars, I added the codes to call overseas. How would you like to call Switzerland?"

Swinging the *Charger* around other cars on the road much too fast, Drummond knew his partner was waiting for him to play the game. "Okay, what happens if I use that number and call the Swiss?"

"Yes. Dial zero-one-one-four-one and these other nine numbers, and a very polite man will answer. They speak several languages, including English. It's one of those banks where security and secrecy is important."

Watching the road, Drummond nodded. "So, we've found a big chunk of Wilmor's money. But how do we get it out of that vault? The Swiss might be very polite, but they're also very stubborn when it comes to funds in their hands."

They were pulling in behind the police headquarters. By the time they were up in their office, Hermon had convinced

Drummond of how to get the Swiss bank to release the funds. Releasing the funds would shut down Wilmor. Anything that involved the government of a country, the Swiss were very good at co-operating. The partners needed to prove that Morrison was dirty and connected to Wilmor.

What they did for the next few shifts was search. While Hermon did a lot of illegal hacks, Drummond was going through a lot of files. Some of the files were from the stacks on the back table. Other files were from what Hermon was finding, and they were being forwarded or faxed from other departments or other cooperative out-of-state police information centers. It was the slow police work that all good cops were trained to do, and not all had the patience to perform. These two were like penned-up bulldogs, digging a hole under the fence. They weren't going to give up until they found the answer.

Then, like all puzzles, all it took was one small answer to bring the whole house tumbling down. Among the receipts from Wilmor's aide at Bildof Investments was a receipt for some unusual chemicals. A call to the company that shipped the items identified the chemicals as a plastic explosive known as C-4. They brought the aide in and threatened her with a long time in jail for the possession of banned dangerous materials. She cried and then talked about a man that Mr. Wilmor had instructed her would pick up the package late one day in the office.

They next shift had a rough-looking gentleman by the current name of Ralph Montero in a holding cell. Taking his time for the interrogation and with an Assistant DA along to make a deal that would keep the guy from the death sentence — they got a lot of details. They had the bomber tied directly back to Wilmor. In exchange, he gave up the name of a gentleman who had a habit of breaking people's necks for the right price.

Days later, Hermon was entering information into his

computer, and Drummond was again making deals with a gentleman named Diamond Tooth Charley Thompson. The black gentleman also had some information to exchange to avoid the death sentence. It seemed he'd been sent out of state to do some dirty work for a guy that needed some competition eliminated. He was willing to avoid the needle in order to testify about who the competition was against. Now, the partners called in the US government and dumped it all in their lap, including the Swiss bank's funds.

Months later, as Drummond and Hermon worked on a simple death, they were watching the news about a representative in a nearby state being arrested for crimes. It was also announced that large amounts of gold were handed over by the Swiss government to the US government based on crimes connected with a government representative affixed to a crime spree.

Hermon looked up for the news and smiled. "Hey, partner, how about taking the night off? I want to spend some time with my wife."

"You know what, that sounds great. I know a lady with a great pair of legs and a whole bunch of cats that I've promised to help sort out and find homes for. I need some downtime. Who knows what's going to pop up next?"

The End

ABOUT THE AUTHOR

The author lives in Florida, and under the pen name of M. Garnet (Muriel Garnet Yantiss), spends all her time writing, reading, or talking to writers and readers.

Writing SciFi, Fantasy, and Romance. Her web site is www.mgarnet.com to show all the books she has written.

You can find her on Amazon on her Author's website at https://www.amazon.com/author/m.garnet

If you would like a free book and get on M. Garnet's mailing list, send your email address to her at mgarnet2@yahoo.com.

Put in a word where you found this book to let others know how you liked this story. Thanks.